IN TOO DEEP

BATH PAPADAKIS : BOOK 9

LONDON CRIME THRILLER SERIES

CARA ALEXANDER

Copyright © 2023 by Cara Alexander

All rights reserved.

No part of this book may be reproduced in any form or by any electronic or mechanical means, including information storage and retrieval systems, without written permission from the author, except for the use of brief quotations in a book review.

This is a work of fiction. Names, characters, organizations, places, events, and incidents are either products of the author's imagination or are used fictitiously.

EXCLUSIVE OFFER

To instantly receive a free copy of the prequel, **Break Up**, sign up for Cara Alexander's free newsletter at...
www.caraaalexander.com

ALSO BY CARA ALEXANDER

Followed
The Killing
Panic
Payback
Pure Evil
Fallout
Fatal Intent
Nemesis
In Too Deep
Hidden From View

PROLOGUE

HAMPSTEAD
North London 8.30am

JULIA'S PHONE rings as she walks towards Hampstead tube.

Digging in her bag for her phone, she glances at the number and a shiver runs down her spine. *It's him again.*

Last night she said wasn't going to do it anymore — he said if she didn't he'd leak everything to the press.

She stops walking and looks at her still ringing phone.

If he says he wants me to do it, I'll just hang up.

'Yes?'

'It's me—I'll be waiting in the same place today and you'd better have what I asked you for.'

'No, I'm not doing it anymore.'

Shoving her phone back into her bag, she grits her teeth and walks into Hampstead station.

As usual, it's busy. The board says she has three minutes

to wait till her train comes, so time to walk to the end of the platform where she knows the train won't be so busy.

This is her routine every day — she places herself at the edge of the platform exactly where the doors will open so she has a chance of getting a seat.

An advert showing a woman in a red bikini with long blond hair running along a sandy beach is on the wall opposite her. *If only I could go somewhere far away from here. I must think of a way to get him to stop...* She breaks out into a cold sweat and grips her bag tightly. If only she hadn't agreed to do it.

The loud rumbling of the oncoming train through the London tunnel snaps her out of it and she gets ready to leap inside the train when the door's open.

Suddenly she feels a push on her lower back.

What...

It happens again, but this time it's harder — she tries to stop herself, but she's in the air...

They don't even hear her scream as the oncoming train hits her.

Screams of horror fill the air as the people who were standing next to her see her falling in front of the train — the train driver puts on his brakes, but it's too late...

Panic ripples through the crowded Tube station as word gets around of what's just happened. Security guards appear running towards the platform, but it's too late for Julia.

One of them shouts, 'Oh my god we need an ambulance quickly.'

Another security guard looks at the crowded platform where people still gaze at the scene in front of them in horror. She tries to calm them down, but they're traumatized and terrified and desperate to get out of the station. Some start running for the elevators — some for the steps.

This is the deepest station on the London underground with over 320 steps to climb to get out.

People stand holding onto each other, weeping. Police cars and ambulances squeal to a halt outside the station and then the grizzly task of recovering poor Julia from under the train begins.

1

TWO WEEKS EARLIER

A WOMAN and a man leave a restaurant. The man draws the woman to him, caresses her face, kisses her, then mumbles, 'Let's get a cab...'

Then a man walking towards them suddenly stops right in front of them and stands looking at the woman.

'Julia, is that you?'

The woman looks at him. It's someone she used to know at university.

He smiles. 'Aren't you going to introduce me?'

Julia looks annoyed, then mutters. 'This is someone I knew at university...' Her voice trails off as she looks at Allen standing next to her — he doesn't look very happy.

'Jake, my name is Jake,' says the man, ignoring Julia's discomfort and holding out his hand. 'Nice to meet you.'

Then he looks at him closely. 'Don't I know you?'

IN TOO DEEP

Allen hesitates, then shakes his head. 'Sorry, I don't think we've met.'

Jake looks at him again, then laughs. 'Of course, I've seen you on TV — you're Allen Marshall, the CEO of that stocks and shares company...'

'Jake,' the woman snaps. Then, in a softer voice, adds. 'We're in a hurry. It was nice seeing you.'

'Yes, you, too.'

A cab draws up and whisks the couple away.

Jake legs it to his nearby car and follows the cab.

Allen turns to Julia sitting beside him. 'Is he someone you dated?'

'We were at university together, that's all.'

Hampstead
North London

Two hours later, a cab draws up outside an elegant townhouse in London's Hampstead in North London.

Julia pays the driver, slides out of the cab, then spots Jake waiting outside the high walled townhouse.

'What are you doing here?' she asks, walking over to where he's standing watching her.

'I think you know, don't you?'

She shakes her head. 'No, why are you here?'

'I followed you in my car to that hotel, Julia. I took lots of photos of you and him with your arms around each other going into room 707 of Olympia Hotel. Not a luxury hotel by any stretch of the imagination, but I guess you must be care-

7

ful. They would notice people in his position in grander establishments, wouldn't they?'

He pauses and waits for what he's saying to sink in. She flinches, but stares at him defiantly.

'So what?'

'Come on Julia, the scarf he put on before you walked inside the hotel that covered his face...'

Julia's face flushes. 'Shut it, Jake. What do you want?'

'Just some information.'

'Get lost.'

She goes to shove him aside, but he pulls her back close to him, inhales her expensive perfume and in a chill voice he murmurs. 'The room next door to the one you went in was empty and lucky for me; the walls are very thin.'

Taking out his phone, he turns the volume up, holds it to her ear and watches as the shock slowly spreads across her face.

She goes to grab his phone. He grasps her wrist with his other hand.

'Stop it, you're hurting me.'

Without taking his eyes off her face, he puts his phone back into his pocket, then smiles. 'All the grunts and groans and the *Oh Julia - Oh Allen...*'

She pushes past him.

He pulls her back.

'Not so fast. If you don't want hubby to know who you're screwing, then you must do something for me.'

She says nothing.

He smiles. 'Don't worry, all I want is a little information. It should be easy, as you're his personal assistant in more ways than one, aren't you?'

A light goes on in the front room of the house, casting a

silvery shadow from the door to the entrance of the gate near the wall where they're standing.

Julia quickly walks away, opens the gate, and goes inside.

Her husband Duncan's holding a glass of wine chatting on his phone. As soon as he sees her he ends the call and saunters over to the kitchen.

'Who was that?' Julia asks, noticing how flushed he is.

'Oh, just work.'

The kitchen door is open and through the door she sees him refilling his glass from a bottle of white wine.

She knows what happens when he drinks too much — they always have a row.

Walking into the bedroom, she slips on her nightie, and lays down.

But Duncan has other things on his mind than Julia tonight and hopes she'll go to sleep quickly.

He has a high-profile job but doesn't confide in her anymore, something which irritates her intensely. They've been married for two years and since the birth of their one-year-old child, their sex life is practically zero. The days of extended foreplay and a snuggle after a long session of making love are well and truly gone.

She hinted at getting a divorce saying their sex life was nonexistent and ended up having an enormous row.

He adamantly refused, saying it would jeopardize his chances of getting on in government. Plus, his family is deeply religious, so they're against divorce. However, that doesn't stop him sneaking off to the *au pair's* room when she's asleep, which is exactly what he does now.

As usual Amelia's on her bed waiting for him when he opens the door.

'Is she asleep?' she murmurs.

'Yes, she's asleep and snoring like a pig, as usual.'

Amelia laughs. 'Poor Duncan.'

Duncan goes over to her, slips her nightdress strap down and starts fondling her breasts.

'Oh Duncan,' Amelia murmurs, wriggling with delight.

Soon the nightdress is laying on the floor.

An hour later, Duncan's back in his bedroom.

JULIA SUSPECTS their new *au pair,* Amelia listens to what's going on in their bedroom when they row, as she always has a sly smile on her face when she sees her in the morning. She also suspects her husband's screwing her.

Once, when she came home early, she caught Amelia in her bra and pants outside their bedroom door. To say she was angry is putting it mildly.

Amelia ran to her bedroom. Julia opened their bedroom door and confronted her husband, who was laying naked on the bed.

Her face was red with fury. 'Don't take me for a fool Duncan, you were having it off with her, weren't you?'

He groaned making Julia even more angry.

'Don't groan at me, she was outside our bedroom door practically naked,'

'How should I know why the stupid creature walks around half naked?'

Then he covered himself with the duvet and muttered something under his breath.

'What did you say?'

'Julia darling, why would I fuck that creature when I have you?'

That's when she decided to accept the invitation from her boss, Allen, to go for a drink after work. He's a bit of a womanizer, but he's not bad looking and what's good for the goose is good for the gander.

2

BETH AT HOME
   7.30am

I'M in the kitchen making a coffee when my phone rings. It's Elias.

'Good morning, Elias you're up early or haven't you been to bed yet?'

'You forget Beth, we're two hours ahead here in Greece.'

I grunt and pour the hot coffee into my mug. 'So how are you?'

'Busy as usual, I'm covering a story about the…'

He pauses, then carries on talking. 'Look Beth, I need to talk to you. It's about Alex.'

'What about Alex?'

'It's about his assets.'

'Assets?'

'Yes, Beth, his business, bank account—apartment—the police have frozen all his assets. They'll be contacting you soon. I'm sorry to call so early, but I wanted you to know before they tell you.'

I stand staring at my coffee, then quietly ask. 'How do you know?'

'Beth, you forget I have contacts in the police. It hasn't hit the papers yet, but when it does...'

My coffee's now forgotten as I pace around the kitchen with my arms wrapped around me. 'I can't believe this!' I mutter. 'He wasn't an angel, but he worked for that money. When he first started out with that law firm, he was working all hours just to make the business work. We both sacrificed to get it going, we...'

'Yes, Beth, I know, but try to focus on what's happening now. He worked for Limonides and you know what he's like, and he isn't the only millionaire with dubious dealings Alex worked for. From what I've heard, Alex was aiding many like him with their criminal activities.'

'Who, Elias, do you know?'

'Oh, come on Beth, where do you think Alex got all that money from?'

Gritting my teeth, I walk over to the window and open it. 'Is Limonides also under investigation? Has he had his assets frozen?'

'I'm not sure I'll find out, but this is just the tip of the iceberg. Corruption in high places rarely catches up with those who've gained so much from it but now...'

'So, his account, our apartment, his business...'

'Yes, they're all frozen and it could take months, even years, for them to investigate everything and everyone Alex was involved with.'

'Is there anything else you're not telling me?'

'No Beth, and if I find out anything, I'll let you know

immediately. I'm sorry I had to be the bearer of such bad news.'

Just as I let out a groan, Mum comes into the kitchen. She takes one look at my face and mouths - *What's wrong?*

Covering my phone with my hand, I mumble, 'Nothing, I'll tell you later.'

She raises an eyebrow and leaves the room.

As soon as the door closes behind her, I mutter. 'How long is this going to take?'

'I don't know — I'm not a lawyer. Maybe Dev can help. He's a qualified criminal lawyer.'

'I can't ask him.'

He's about to say something, then stops. 'Is everything alright between you two?'

I sigh. 'Yes.'

'Do you want me to speak to him?'

'No, it's okay. Thanks Elias, thanks for letting me know.'

'Well, if you need to talk, you know where I am. Now I must get down to the police station.'

'Is it about Alex?'

'I'll call you later, Beth, and if they call you and ask anything, just say you don't know.'

I sit staring out of the window, then my phone rings.

It's Dev.

'Beth, sorry to call so early, but we need to talk. Your phone was busy. Was it work?'

'No, it was Elias. I must get ready, or I'll be late for work. I'll tell you later.'

'Can't you tell me now?'

'No, I'll call you later, Dev.'

He inhales quickly, then mutters. 'Okay, call me.'

I head for the shower.

The warm pulsating water on my back relaxes me, and I

IN TOO DEEP

start thinking of Jamie. He's going to Athens for a few weeks. The school said he can go, but only for a few weeks. I know he's not thrilled to be here in London, and if I live with Dev, it can't be here, so we'll have to move, but what about my job?

Then I think of our apartment in Athens. It's where Jamie grew up, it's home to him, but the news about Alex will be on the TV and in the papers, so he's sure to find out, if not from the TV, then from one of his friends. I'll just have to tell Jamie what's happened otherwise he'll wonder why they're not staying at our place.

Turning off the shower, I grab a towel, rub myself dry and quickly get dressed, all the time thinking about Jamie, Alex, and our apartment in Athens.

3

BETH
Bayswater
London

'Your phone's ringing,' shouts Mum from the kitchen.

Turning off the shower, I grab a towel, run into the bedroom, but as soon as I pick it up it stops ringing.

It's an Athens number. It's not Elias, it's Helen.

I sit, rubbing myself dry on my bed. I must make this short, otherwise I'll be late and I'm not giving Hardcastle any more ammunition to get rid of me. I sometimes wonder why I put myself through all this shit...

I press Helen's number — she picks up.

'Beth, I'm sorry to call you so early. I know you're probably getting ready for work, but...'

'Yes, I am Helen. Can I call you back or is it urgent?'

She gives a little sigh. 'Why are you still slogging away at that job, Beth?'

'Do you really think I want to? Do you think I enjoy working all hours just to get a story?'

Now she's laughing. 'Yes, Beth, you do.' Then she sounds serious. 'If you needed the money, I could understand, but you don't.'

Silence.

'We're not here for long, so why not make the most of it and be happy?'

'For your information, Helen, I don't have any money.'

'Oh, come on Beth, Alex left you a fortune and a business and your apartment.'

'No, Helen. The police have put a freeze on all his money and assets.'

'Why?'

'Working for people with criminal intent. Allowing people, drugs and who knows what to enter the country.'

Silence.

I carry on. 'It seems Limonides was not the only person getting legal favors from Alex. It appears he was helping people like Limonides for a long time, so...'

'But your apartment — it's half yours.'

'Yes, but it was also half Alex's.'

'I'm so sorry Beth.'

'Look I must go Helen.'

'Yes, of course.'

'Was it anything urgent?'

'No, I'll call later.'

I quickly get dressed, thinking about Jamie, Alex, and our apartment in Athens. Mum loves having Jamie stay with her and I think she'd rather be there than in our apartment.

Mum's in the living room as usual with her coffee watching the news.

I'm just about to tell her what's happened when she turns and sees me. She points to the TV.

Following her eyes, I look at the crowds of people outside Hampstead Tube station.

'What happened?'

'A woman was pushed under a train.'

My phone rings. It's Fred.

'Get down here quickly Beth, we've got a VIP story to cover.'

'Don't you want me to meet you outside the Tube?'

'What are you talking about?'

'The woman, the one who was just shoved under a train on the underground. It's on the news.'

'No, come here as quickly as you can.'

He hangs up.

I grab my bag. 'See you later, Mum.'

'Is it about this?' she asks, pointing to the TV screen.

I shrug. 'I'll call you later, Mum.'

Then I stop. 'Where is Jamie?'

'He went to school early, so don't worry about him.'

'Did you take him?'

'Yes, I was up at six.'

'Why was he up so early?'

'He has a lot to do before we leave for Athens.'

I return to the living room and stand looking at her.

'Yes, Beth, we're going to Athens in a few days and there's still time for you to get a ticket and come with us.'

I groan. 'I have a job to go to, Mum.'

'Yes, I know. But you also have an apartment in Athens and enough money—'

I wasn't going to tell her, but...

'Elias called me this morning about Alex's bank account. They've frozen everything, Mum.'

Her eyes open wide. 'But they can't!'

'Unfortunately, it seems they can, and they've also put a freeze on his business and the apartment.'

'But it's yours.'

'Half, it's in both our names.'

She sits staring at me. 'What about Jamie? He thinks we're going to stay there.'

'Don't worry, Mum, I'm sure they'll sort it out. I'll talk to him. Now I really must go.'

It's early so the journey on the Tube doesn't take long plus with what's on the news, I think it's stopped many people from taking the Tube to work. Many are now going by bus or walking.

Fortunately, the train line I'm on isn't affected, but many are. I change at the next stop, then I'm out of the Tube heading for the news building where I work.

My colleague Fred's always desperate for a coffee, so I pop into Costa for our early morning fix, then head for the elevator.

4

NEWSROOM

FRED LOOKS up as I enter the newsroom.

'Is one of those coffees for me?' he asks, licking his lips.

'Now why would I buy you a coffee?' I mutter, placing both on my desk as I sit down and open my laptop.

He walks over, pulls up a chair, sniffs the fresh coffee, and looks at me. 'I smell something fishy...'

Fred often comes out with unusual stuff like this — it's the way his mind works.

Popping open the lid of one coffee, I lean back in my chair, take a sip, then lean forward and push the other cup towards him. 'Of course, it's for you, and I can assure you there's nothing fishy about it.'

His green eyes glint mischievously as he flips open the polystyrene top of the cup and gulps down a few mouthfuls of the hot coffee. 'Who said I was referring to the coffee?'

'So, what's fishy?'

He sits staring ahead, gulping down his coffee.

'Has Hardcastle been stuffing himself with fish and chips again in here? Was he working late last night?'

'Don't be silly,' he scoffs. 'Old Hardcastle's not a fish and chips man, maybe he used to be, but now he enjoys the finer delights of dining.'

Shrugging, I place my empty cup on my desk. 'So, if it's not him, what is it?'

Getting up, he walks over to the window, throws the empty cup into the bin, walks over to me and motions to my laptop.

'Look at Hardcastle's email. He wants us to go to Billingsgate fish market as soon as possible. Seems there's a dead body in a box of frozen fish.'

Frowning, I open his email:

Get down to Billingsgate Market before the others. I'll see you there.

H

'If it's so urgent, why didn't he call or text me?' I mutter.

Fred sighs. 'He called me at six twenty this morning and told me to call you, then get down here and take you with me.'

'Why not meet me there?'

Fred shrugs. 'Who knows how his mind works?'

Leaning close to me, he whispers. 'Maybe he has CCTV in this place and wants to check we're here on time. He's probably listening to us now.'

I sit thinking about the horrific killing of a woman on the Tube this morning. Surely that's the story we should be covering.

He smiles. 'I know what you're thinking, Beth.'

'You do?'

He nods. 'I thought the same after I saw the newsflash earlier, but we're going to Billingsgate market not the Tube station.'

His phone rings. He answers, then looks at me.

'The cab's downstairs. Come on.'

WE SLIDE into the back of the blue Uber car and head towards Canary Wharf –- financial hub of the city of London and home to Billingsgate Fish Market.

'Did you know the market gets its name from a ward in the south-east corner of the City of London?'

Fred frowns. 'Where are you going with this?'

'Just sharing information, Fred. I thought you'd like a background on where we're going.'

'And you think I don't know?'

'Do you?'

He grunts. 'The original fish market was by the river. Then they moved it here. It's a bit like Covent Garden Market, but the other way round. That market used to be in the center of London, then they moved it near to Vauxhall.'

'Yeah, Mum said the pubs near Covent Garden Market were open all night for the workers. If you were up late, you could always pop in for a drink and buy fresh fruit and flowers. It's a shame they moved it over near the river in Vauxhall.'

He turns and looks at me. 'Were you born in London?'

'Yes.'

'And what about your mum?'

'She was born in Cornwall but spent most of her life

living in London. Then when she met dad, she lived in Greece.'

'They're not together now, are they?'

'No.'

He's about to say something, then thinks better of it and looks out of the cab window.

Fred's always talking about his French side and how he used to live in France. I'm just about to ask him if he was born in London when he blurts out.

'Are you going back to live in Athens soon?'

Taken a little aback by his question, I shrug.

Shall I tell him what Elias told me this morning about Alex's assets being frozen?

But before I can, he cranes his neck out of the window, then waffles on about Canary Wharf.

'Canary Wharf has the tallest glass buildings I've seen in London and some of the best pubs and restaurants.'

'The food's good?'

'Yes, I used to go to a place when I was working around here. Great big juicy steaks and...'

'Shut it, Fred.'

'Sorry, I forgot you don't partake of the flesh.'

We sit silently staring at the tall glass buildings.

Then he mutters. 'It's a little early for the city slickers to glide in front of us in their fitted suits and posh haircuts. This is a city that never sleeps, Beth. Some work late, but it's the cleaners who come here every night to make it look sparkling clean for the next day's financial catastrophe or cause for yet another celebration and popping of corks of *Don Perignon*. I'll bet they've got lots of stories they could tell us.'

'Yeah, but it takes its toll on some of the so-called city slickers.'

He laughs. 'Yeah, they get paid too much, drink too much and get drunk too much.'

'No, seriously. I remember recently there was a story that didn't make it to the headlines which was very sad. A young guy who worked here jumped from one of those tall glass buildings.'

'He must have got in too deep with something. Probably ended up at one of those parties, had too much to drink and topped himself.'

I stare up at the tall glass buildings and shudder. 'What a terrible way to go.'

5

BILLINGSGATE FISH MARKET
Canary Wharf, London

FRED STOPS GAWPING at the buildings and looks at me. 'What time does Billingsgate Market close?'

'I'm not sure. They usually open very early, so probably don't stay open late.'

The Uber driver in the front turns and flashes us a smile. 'It opens at 4.00am and closes at 8.30am in the morning. Sundays for shellfish only from 6 - 8am. Monday it's closed.

Fred gives me one of his mischievous grins.

'You come here often, then?' he asks.

'I live near here.'

The Uber driver slows down, then points to a large sign saying City of London Billingsgate Market.

'This is the market.'

As we scramble out Fred looks around.

I walk over to where he's standing and look for the police or Hardcastle.

'Hardcastle said he'd meet us here, so where is he?'

Fred shrugs. 'Let's talk to the workers and police and get the lowdown on what happened. The police will have it cordoned off by now, so it should be easy to find. Come on, maybe we'll get there before he does.'

Fred's walking so fast I must run to keep up with him.

'Slow down,' I mutter.

He ignores me.

I stop running and glare at him.

He slows down. 'Sorry, I just can't stand the smell of fish.'

'But you love to eat it.'

He groans.

'Look Fred, I've been thinking. They send fish to most parts of the country from here, don't they?'

'Yes, they supply all the top restaurants and hotels. This is one of the biggest fish markets in the UK.'

'So, they'll know where this crate of fish was going and where it came from.'

'Of course, and it should be easy to find out, as everything's done digitally, even here. Now let's go over to where that crowd's gathering it must be where the police and the crate are.'

As we get closer, I hear many of the onlookers whispering and nodding to where the police have erected a temporary tent and made it a crime scene.

A police officer walks over to us as we duck under the police cordon and walk towards the crime scene.

'Nobody's allowed in here,' he snaps. 'Stand over there.'

We both flash our reporter cards.

He grunts. 'You still have to wait over there.'

Fred ignores him and looks over to where the police are. A woman's hovering near the crate and talking to someone dressed in working clothes.

His eyes light up. 'It's PC Donnelly. It must be our lucky day.'

Fred walks closer. The officer goes to grab him, but he slips away.

'PC Donnelly,' he calls, running over to where she's standing.

People turn their heads.

She looks up, sees us, shakes her head, then turns to the police officer. 'It's alright, they can come through.'

They have cordoned the entire area off with police tape and a temporary cover made around the crate. We stand looking at the half open crate of frozen fish.

'How long have you been here?' I ask, walking closer to the crate.

'About thirty minutes. Forensics have just finished taking samples.'

PC Donnelly turns to the worker she was talking with. 'These two are friends of mine. They're reporters.'

He doesn't seem to hear his eyes are on the crate. 'I thought there was something fishy about it,' he mutters.

Fred covers his mouth, trying to suppress a laugh.

Giving him one of my looks to shut him up, I turn to the man, who looks deeply troubled.

'Why is that?'

'I've worked here long enough to know how much they weigh, and this crate was bloody heavy. That's why I peeked inside.'

He describes what he saw when a voice behind us makes us jump.

'Glad to see you got here quickly. Did you find anything?'

Fred looks from the crate to Hardcastle, who's eying us, then points to the man who was just recounting what had happened.

'Seems this market worker opened that crate containing oysters and at the bottom he saw a curled-up figure with a bottle of Bollinger champagne shoved...'

'Fred!' snaps PC Donnelly.

Fred shrugs. 'Where the sun don't shine.'

Hardcastle raises an eyebrow.

Fred mutters. 'Well, at least they sent him off in style.'

'Why do you say that?' asks Hardcastle.

Fred looks surprised. 'Champagne and oysters, the *fayre* of the rich I thought you'd have known that?'

Hardcastle's eyes glint. 'Trying to be cheeky, are we?'

Fred ignores him, then as an afterthought he adds. 'There must be a meaning or a message to it.'

Hardcastle snorts. 'You mean like there's a message inside that bottle?'

Fred can't resist a laugh. 'No, I mean why waste a bottle of Bolly by shoving it up his... you know what?'

He stops and looks at us.

'What significance is there in doing that?'

He walks over to where the frozen corpse is and stares at the bottle.

'Maybe to disrespect him,' I mutter, looking at the grotesque scene in front of me.

Fred's eyes light up. 'Of course, what could be more hideous? I wonder if he was alive when they did it?'

The sound of voices coming from the corridor stops Fred in his tracks. He walks closer to Hardcastle. 'Who gave you the tip off? I mean, this happened a couple of hours ago. Maybe longer.'

Hardcastle taps the side of his nose. 'One of my contacts, a very good contact and I'm not telling you who it is.'

PC Donnelly looks at Hardcastle and frowns. 'When notified about this, we were told nobody knew about it, so I'd love to know where your information came from?'

He ignores her.

'So, what now?' Fred asks.

'We're waiting for a report from forensics.'

'You didn't say where the crate came from?' PC Donnelly says, looking at the fish worker who's still standing behind her.

'Most of it's freshly caught in places like Cornwall, Scotland, and brought by lorry overnight.'

'So not from abroad?'

Hardcastle's eyebrows shoot up. 'Fish is fish, unless you mean...'

PC Donnelly nods. 'Yes, fish you can't get in these waters.'

Hardcastle grunts, takes out his phone and texts someone.

A second later, he gets a reply.

'Transported from Heathrow Airport early this morning.'

'Where from?' I ask.

Hardcastle snorts. 'I don't know he's finding out.'

'Who is?' Fred asks.

'The guy I just spoke to.'

Fred sighs. 'And when will he know?'

Hardcastle eyes him. 'I don't know. He's got to track it.'

Fred shrugs, then looks at Hardcastle. 'It's all done digitally. He only has to look at a computer to find out.'

Hardcastle ignores him. 'Now, as I was saying, forensics will give us all the info we need.'

He looks over at the crate, sighs, then walks away.

Then he stops, turns around and shouts. 'Hang around and find out what you can and send me an update within the hour so I can get it in the next edition.'

6

LATER THAT DAY

DEV HOLDS me at arm's length, his blue eyes glint but not with mischief more like impatience.

'Beth, I said I'm not going to wait long. I need to know if we're going to be together or not?'

I sigh and return his gaze.

'You know I'm worried about Jamie — he needs more time. He just lost his dad.'

Dev lets go of me, turns, and heads for the door.

'Where are you going?'

He swings round and glares at me. 'Do you really care, Beth? You have a son who I think likes me. I know he's just lost his dad, but he wasn't living here. In fact, he hardly ever saw him. I thought we…'

'That's not fair, Dev. You know I care. It's just not the right time. Surely you understand that?'

'No Beth, I don't.'

The front door slams shut behind him. I run to the window, open it, and watch as he leaves the block entrance. He usually turns and gives me a wave, but not this time.

Sliding into his black BMW, he speeds off down the street. Then he stops, reverses back, opens his window and shouts, 'If you change your mind, let me know, but it's got to be quick.'

I stand staring at him, then he's gone.

A few hours later, I get a text from Dev.
I'll call you when I'm back.
Dev
My reply:
Where are you going?
His reply:
I think you know.

I'M in the park taking a walk, which always seems to calm me down when my phone rings.

It's Elias.

'Elias, how are things in Athens?'

'Okay, but I'm worried about Helen. I called her yesterday and there was no reply. I was passing her business just now and popped in to see how she was, but there's a closed sign on the door.'

'I wouldn't worry, Elias. When she called me, she sounded fine. Maybe she has a new boyfriend and is just having a few days off from work.'

'I hope so. It's just not like her to go somewhere without telling me. I always monitor her house and business if she's away.'

'She's lucky to have you, Elias, but don't worry, I'll get her to call you immediately if I hear from her.'

'Thanks Beth, I just want to know she's somewhere safe, then I won't worry.'

Talking to Elias makes me think of Dev. I press his number — it goes to voicemail.

What's wrong with me? I just spoke to him...

I hate it when he leaves like this. Of course, I want to be with him, but Jamie's going through a bad time right now — his dad just died and now is not the time for us to start living together.

Taking out my phone, I call Elias.

'Elias.'

'Beth, any news?'

'No, I'm calling about Dev. Do you know where he might be going on his next trip?'

'But I thought he was still in London.'

I won't tell Elias that I think he's already gone, so say. 'I just thought he might have told you.'

'Why don't you call him and ask him?'

I say nothing.

'Are you two alright, has something happened?'

Shall I confide in Elias and tell him what's wrong?

I decide against it, you never know he might tell Dev.

I sigh. 'No, everything's okay.'

'Have you thought of anywhere Helen might be or where she would go?'

'In Athens?'

'Yes. Anyone you know she might stay with?'

'You're really worried, aren't you?'

'Yes, since our last little escapade when you were here in Athens, Helen and I often meet for a drink or have a coffee. I don't think she's as happy here as she used to be.'

'Yes, I know what you mean.'

I don't say it, but I know Helen hates bumping into her ex on the streets of Athens. That's why I moved after Alex, and I split up. I think of Alex and the last time I was in Athens...

'Beth, are you still there?'

'Sorry, Elias, I was thinking. I'll call you back later.'

7

NEXT DAY

I'M JUST ABOUT to leave for work when Mum shouts.

'Beth, come and see what's on TV.'

Popping my head around the door, I see plastered on the bottom of the TV screen.

MINISTER ACCUSED OF MURDER

People hold placards high in the chilly morning sky are chanting...

Sack Ballantyne-Smythe

One placard has black writing saying...

END THE SLEAZE
GET RID OF BALLANTYNE - SMYTHE

Another says...

WE WANT JUSTICE

'That poor young woman,' Mum murmurs, looking at the screen. 'I never liked him, you could tell what he was like just to look at him.'

'I don't understand?'

She looks at me sharply. 'I thought you, of all people, would have known about this. They must have proof otherwise they wouldn't demonstrate, would they?'

'What proof do they have?' I ask, staring at those chanting and waving placards outside No 10 Downing Street.

'Well, for one, that poor woman's sister said Julia told her he was having an affair with the *au pair*. She caught her in her bra and pants outside their bedroom door. '

'Where did you hear this?'

'She was being interviewed on TV. When Julia confronted her husband, he just laughed it off and said, what's it to do with him if the stupid creature wants to run around half naked?'

'Not very nice.'

Mum nods. 'He has a reputation as a womanizer.'

'Yes, but to call him a murderer, they need more proof than that. The CCTV cameras on the platform picked up the figure of someone wearing a black hoodie behind the woman. They don't know if someone pushed her, or she jumped. She could have been so desperate she wanted to end it all.'

Mum looks at me in surprise. 'Yes, but they caught her husband on CCTV close to Hampstead tube station, not long after it happened.'

'Was he wearing a black hoodie?'

'No, of course not.'

'And they have this on CCTV?'

'They have him walking along the street not far away from where it happened.'

'Yes, but did they actually see him go into a toilet and change?'

Mum raises an eyebrow. 'No, I'm just saying what could have happened. If it wasn't him then who was it? I'm not sure if they caught anyone wearing a black hoodie outside the station on CCTV.'

She gets up and stops. 'You should check the CCTV. Maybe you can identify who did it.'

'Mum, many people wear black hoodies. The police must have interviewed all the people who were standing next to her and asked if they have any information on this. Have they shown anything like that on the TV?'

She shrugs. 'I've seen none of those on the platform being interviewed, only her sister and that was outside her house. Poor thing, how the press hounds them. I felt sorry for her. What she must be going through — it's terrible. Many of those on the platform were going to work. As soon as they saw what happened they must've made a dash for the lift or the stairs of which there are many in Hampstead tube station.' She pauses. 'Didn't you go down there when Fred called you?'

'No, we're covering another story.'

She looks surprised but says nothing.

8

NEXT DAY
 Mum & Jamie go to Athens...

WHILE I'M GETTING ready to take Mum and Jamie to the airport, Mum's checking they have everything.

'Jamie, hurry. We must leave soon for the airport.'

'Coming Nan, just looking for something to take with me.'

Mum looks at me. 'Sure, you don't want to come?'

'I wish I could, but I have a job.'

She sighs, walks back into the living room. I finish making a drink for Jamie, then take a sip of my coffee and think of what Jamie's going back to.

He's still in shock after losing his dad. I never thought it would happen to Alex. I sit thinking about the good times when we first met and how hard he worked to get that law business going. He was different then, he was always there for Jamie, and he was always there for me until...'

'Your phone's ringing in the living room, Beth. If you're taking us to the airport, you'd better hurry.'

I run into the living room, grab my phone from the table. It's Fred. I'm just about to tell him I'm taking Mum and Jamie to the airport when he mutters.

'I just received a call from Hardcastle. We're no longer covering the fish market murder.'

'Why?'

'I don't know Beth, he just said he wants us to cover what happened at Hampstead Tube.'

'Who's covering the fish market murder?'

'He didn't say.'

'But no other paper has covered it — it doesn't make sense.'

'Tell me about it.'

'Do you think he's been told to keep it out of the news for a while?'

Fred gives a cynical laugh. 'You mean he's up to his old tricks again?'

'Could be.'

'Listen Beth, I've booked an Uber to take us to see DCI Stuart Johnson, he must know something about it as Hampstead's his neck of the woods. In fact, their police station is just a few minutes from the station where it happened.'

'But Fred...'

'I know it's early, but he's busy, so I had to agree to go now.'

'I can't. I'm taking Mum and Jamie to the airport. They're going to Athens.'

Fred groans. 'Shit, I forgot about that.'

'We're leaving now. I'll drop them off then drive to Hampstead, I might be a bit late, but other than changing the time...'

'With all that traffic, you'll definitely be late,' mutters Fred.

'Get him to change the time, then.'

'But he said it's the only time he has free today.'

Now he's really pissing me off.

'Fred. Mum, and Jamie are waiting for me. I said I'd take them to the airport, and I am. Surely you don't expect me to tell them to get an Uber?'

'Sorry Beth, it's just that...'

'I'm leaving Fred. Call him, see what he says. Otherwise go by yourself.'

9

BAYSWATER

After parking Mum's old Fiat in the car park around the back of the block, I check my phone to see if Fred's called.

No call. Good, I'll grab some fresh bread from the Greek deli opposite our block, make a quick sandwich, then call Fred.

My phone flashes.

It's a text from Fred.

I'm on my way to your place. I should be there in about fifteen minutes.

With my bag of food from the delicatessen, I run into the entrance of our block, run up the back stairs to our apartment, open the door and run into the kitchen — break a piece off the bread —open the fridge, slap a slice of vegan cheese inside and grab a bottle of sparkling water.

Fifteen minutes later, my sandwich finished, I'm at the window waiting for Fred.

An Uber cab comes to a standstill outside.

Fred looks up at our living room, then opens the cab window.

'Hurry Beth, Stuart's waiting at that pub near the station.'

Two minutes later, I'm in the back seat of the cab, sitting next to him.

'Was everything okay at the airport?' he asks, turning to look at me.

I nod.

Fred catches on quickly. I don't want to talk about it.

He pulls out his phone and flicks through it.

'Do you seriously think something funny's going on, Fred?' I murmur, watching him flick through his emails.

He gives a cynical laugh. 'You mean Hardcastle knows something he's not telling us?'

I nod.

'Who knows? Anyway, we'll soon be at that pub near Stuart's police station — he's sure to know something.'

'The one I went to when I was covering the serial killer case?'

He nods.

'This is strange...'

'I know. For now, we just cover this story and monitor what's happening in Billingsgate. Canary Wharf is one of the most important financial hubs of the city — home to wheeler dealers making millions overnight so it could be related.'

'Exactly,' I mutter. 'That guy could be important, and they're trying to keep it quiet. I mean, how hard is it to find in a matter of seconds where that crate came from? We'll just have to keep track of what's happening in Canary Wharf while we cover the Tube story.'

Fred grins. 'I wonder who Hardcastle's contact is?'

I nod. 'Yeah, if we could find out...'

'Don't worry, we will, but for now we concentrate on the Tube murder.'

'Maybe it was suicide?'

He grunts. 'I don't think so, and neither do you, do you?'

I shrug.

'Beth, Stuart Johnson, owes me one. That's why he agreed to us meeting him. We go back a long time. If we can get something good from him today, we'll be in Hardcastle's good books. He might have something for the next edition, which means...'

'He'll have to let us go back to covering the fish market murder case.'

'Exactly.'

He opens his small mini notebook laptop that he often keeps in his jacket pocket.

'Why do you need that?'

He grins. 'All in good time, Beth.'

'Fred, why someone with your skills risks his life just to get a bloody story which will only last for a day or two till the next one comes along beats me. You could work for GCHQ — you have the skills.'

'GCHQ, the UK's intelligence, security and cyber agency.'

I nod.

He grins. 'Yes, but I enjoy working outside, not sitting in a room all day.'

DCI Stuart Johnson

He's propped up by the bar as usual, facing the pub door — he never has his back to the door and still looks in good shape. Slim but strong, with short blond hair and a boyish face, which he uses to his advantage.

We walk over to him. He nods at Fred, then looks at me. 'Nice to see you, Beth. Glass of wine, coffee?'

'We need to talk,' says Fred.

He smiles. 'So, what'll it be, Beth?'

'*Cafe cortado*.'

He looks at Fred.

'Same for me,' says Fred.

Stuart beckons to the guy behind the bar. 'Two *cafe cortados*.'

The barman nods.

Stuart looks at Fred. 'What do you want to know?'

'It's about the woman killed on the Tube.'

Stuart finishes his coffee, puts the cup down, leans back in his chair and looks at us.

Fred leans forward. 'We need anything you can give us.'

Stuart smiles. 'I had an idea it'd be something like this. Well, you're in luck, because I know something.'

Fred's watching him. 'Go on.'

Stuart grins. 'Someone working in the place where the dead woman worked when interviewed said the woman recently started staying late.'

'Who told you this?'

He taps his nose.

'Come on Stuart, I need a name.'

He sighs and mutters. 'This didn't come from me alright?'

Fred gives him his solemn face look. 'Of course.'

'Orario Odin, she's a cleaner there. Everyone had left, or so she thought. She walked over to collect her cleaning stuff from the kitchen and on her way there she saw Julia Ballantyne-Smythe on one of the boss's laptops.'

'Then what?' I ask.

'Her back was towards the cleaner, but she saw her shove something into the laptop. After a few minutes, she took it out. The cleaner quickly left before Ballantyne-Smythe caught her watching her.'

'She was copying files onto a USB?' Fred mutters.

'Looks like it.'

'Did it happen again?'

'Yes, but in another room doing the same thing.'

'Sounds like she was into something — passing information, but to who? Maybe she got in too deep and that's why...'

Stuart shrugs.

'Why didn't the cleaner say anything?'

'She wasn't sure. Maybe her boss had told her to do this.'

'Any idea what she was copying and what she was doing with it?'

'No.'

'Do you think they killed her because of this?'

'Who knows, maybe she got greedy or maybe she wanted out?'

'Yes, but this is all circumstantial, based on what the cleaner said.'

He nods. 'Yes, but it sounds convincing, don't you think? Woman working late — hadn't done it before.'

He pauses.

Our drinks arrive.

I take a couple of sips from the small cup, then look at

Stuart. 'Did the police ask if any of the staff had noticed her staying late?'

He gives me a sharp look. 'They asked all the routine questions if that's what you mean. Had they noticed anything unusual, out of the ordinary, that sort of thing and nobody had? So, it's only what the cleaner saw. Everyone leaves at 5.00 latest 6.00.' He pauses, looks at his phone, then at us. 'I must go. Do you need a lift?'

Fred looks at me.

Stuart drains his glass of beer. 'Where are you two going?'

'Back to the newsroom.'

'Sorry, I'm going the other way.'

He gets up, collects his phone and keys from the table and murmurs. 'Keep in touch. Anything you find out, let me know first.'

Fred nods. 'Any news from DCI Dawn Dawson?'

His eyebrows shoot up. 'I thought you knew. Her dad passed away. She'll be back after the funeral.'

Fred and I exchange glances.

'How terrible,' I murmur. 'Poor Dawn.'

Stuart nods. 'Yes, very sad.'

Fred frowns. 'That is sad. So, Sofia will go back to...'

'Yes Fred, going back to where she came from. She knew it was only temporary, and I don't think she likes it here, anyway.'

Fred looks surprised. 'I thought she did.'

Stuart shakes his head. 'Don't get me wrong, she's a good detective, but she has her ways, which to some are a bit unusual, to say the least.'

'Like what?' Fred asks, watching me.

'The way she handles people — it's probably the way they taught her, but...'

'She's had it tough,' murmurs Fred, watching him closely.

'Yes, but we all have to cope. None of us have it easy, do we?'

Fred's eyebrows shoot up.

I know what's coming, so before he can say anything I stand up.

'Come on Fred, let's go.'

Then, to my amazement, Stuart gets up and gives me a kiss on the cheek.

'Nice seeing you again, Beth. I'll be in touch.'

He looks at Fred, grins, then walks out of the pub.

10

HAMPSTEAD

'She was getting information for someone about what?' I mutter, as we walk along to the Tube station. 'She worked for a company that deals in stocks and shares, so...'

'That information would come in mighty handy.' Fred adds with a grin.

'Exactly.'

'I don't know, Beth, and if we knew what it was and what she was doing with it, we'd have something for old Hardcastle, but we don't, do we?'

'Seriously Fred, we need to find out about the man she worked for. She was his personal assistant, so she'd have access to all kinds of information. We must check out all the people she worked with, her close friends and her sister.'

Fred raises an eyebrow. 'They're having a field day with this one on the TV — it doesn't stop.'

'What do you mean?'

He doesn't reply, he's flicking through his phone.

'Then there's her husband? Maybe he knows something.'

'Hang on,' groans Fred. 'I've got to reply to old Hardcastle.'

He quickly punches out a reply, then looks at me.

'He's checking on where we are. I told him we're on our way back... Now where were we?'

'Talking about the dead woman's husband.'

'What does he do?' murmurs Fred.

'Works for the government — a minister of health or culture or something. He has a townhouse in Hampstead and a house in the Cotswolds.'

'Don't they all,' mutters Fred, placing his phone in his pocket. 'Not a bad life, is it? A house in the country worth thousands or millions, depending on how big it is. And a four or six million house in Hampstead, London. It makes you wonder where they get all the money from to afford it, doesn't it?'

'He has a high-powered job. In fact, I'm sure he's the Minister of Health.'

Fred's eyes are glinting. 'I'd like to know where they get all the money from to pay for this.'

'Not now Fred, I know how you feel, but we've got to get back to the newsroom, otherwise Hardcastle will have a fit.'

'Okay, when we get back, you do background checks on the murdered woman's husband, and I'll check out his dead wife, Julia. What's the surname?'

'Ballantyne - Smythe.'

Fred smirks, shakes his head, and walks into Hampstead Tube station. I follow.

HARDCASTLE'S not there when we get back to the newsroom, so I check on the husband, Duncan Ballantyne - Smythe.

Fred makes calls to people who can help with information on his dead wife, and his first port of call is DI Sofia Larson.

DI SOFIA LARSON

'Anything about the woman killed on the Tube, Sofia?' Fred asks.

'She was having an affair.'

'How do you know?'

'I've been researching, haven't you?'

'Not really, I was covering another story, then…'

She interrupts. 'Okay, I get it. Her boss deals in stocks and shares, which you probably know, but as well as being his personal assistant, she was also his mistress.' She pauses. 'She was married with a child — a one-year-old.'

Fred's surprised. He'd been flicking through his phone, skimming through all the latest editions of the newspapers, trying to catch up.

'I didn't know that.'

'It hasn't hit the press yet — we only just found out, so do nothing, Fred. Do you understand?'

'Yes, so what happened?'

'I don't know. I'm just trying to piece it together, but from what that cleaner said about seeing her with the USB and on her boss's laptop…'

'But she was having an affair with him.'

'Exactly, so maybe she wasn't taking any information, just trying to keep up to date with her work. Maybe she wanted to impress him. This lot work under a lot of pressure in Canary Wharf.'

Fred sniffs. 'They don't know the meaning of the word.'

'It's not like our work, Fred. I hunt down murderers and you get the story. Take the dead woman's husband, for instance. He works for the government. We're not on the front line like that, are we?'

'What do you mean?'

'Well, running the country.'

'What's his job title?'

'Not sure, but he's a minister of something. I thought you would know that?'

'I told you Hardcastle sent us to cover another story, so we're behind with this one. That's why I need your help in catching up, but from what Beth said, I think he's the minister of health.'

She laughs. 'Just read all those rags they call newspapers; they're having a field day with this one.'

Fred's silent. 'There may be more to it than you think. Don't forget the dead woman was tapping into vital information that if falling into the wrong hands could...'

Now Sofia sounds interested. 'What, Fred?'

'Make them a lot of money — stocks and shares — get it. We must find out what she downloaded onto that USB.'

She sighs. 'Yeah, right Fred, and how do we do that?'

'Is everything alright, Sofia?'

'What do you mean?'

'Well, the job. Working with Stuart Johnson. Do you get on with him?'

'He's okay, a bit of a wanker.'

'Did he try it on with you yet?'

'Look Fred, I really have to go. If you find anything, let me know.'

11

DEV CALLS

I'M at home trying to do some work when my phone rings. It's Dev.

'Dev.'

'Don't sound so surprised. I received a call from Elias saying Helen's missing any idea where she is?'

'No, I told him she called me and sounded alright. I tried calling her but nothing. I left a message at David's hotel in case she was in Spain, but you know what she's like. If she gets a bee in her bonnet about something.'

'Okay.'

'Is that why you called me, Dev?'

'Well, it's important, isn't it?'

'Yes, I just thought...'

'What?'

'Look Dev, I really want us to be together...'

'So do I Beth.'

'Where are you?'

'Somewhere very hot and dangerous.'

Suddenly I feel angry with him. 'Why the hell didn't you stay in Athens?'

'Because they wanted me to come here to do this job. I'm paid to do this. You know that, don't you?'

'But why take something if it's so dangerous?'

Silence.

'Look Dev, I've been thinking. If we took a trip to Cornwall with Jamie, then maybe...'

'What are you saying, Beth?'

'Jamie went on a school trip to Cornwall, and he loved it. He even said he'd like to live there, so maybe we could start something in Cornwall.'

'But Beth, his dad just died, and you said it's too soon for us to be together living in one house.'

'I just thought if we go somewhere different — somewhere he hasn't been before, somewhere near the sea.'

'But what about your apartment, your job — London? Won't you miss it? I remember you said this before when you suggested we become detectives, but what happened? Why didn't we do it then?'

'It was the wrong time, Dev, and you know it.'

He ignores me and carries on. 'You also suggested Brighton. You called it Little London...'

'Yes, it's called that because it's closer to London and that's why I think Cornwall's a better idea. It's far away from London, it's by the sea, it's beautiful and...'

'Have you been there?'

'Yes, my mum's aunt lived there.'

'Beth, consider this carefully. I have a job which I'm committed to and if I give it up...'

'I know Dev and I think this could be good for all of us.'

'Beth, Elias told me about them freezing Alex's assets. Is this why you're doing this, because you can't return to your apartment in Athens?'

Now I'm really getting pissed off.

'I don't care about his money or his business. All I want is the apartment — Jamie wanted to stay there with Mum, and now they can't.'

He grunts. 'Right, well, think carefully, Beth, because Cornwall's an entirely different kettle of fish to London.'

'How do you know?'

'We used to stay there sometimes when I was a child.'

'Did you like it?'

'I was a child, Beth. It was by the sea. Of course, I liked it. Anyway, I must go. I just wanted to find out if Helen was okay.'

'Is that all? You just wanted to find out about Helen?'

'Oh Beth, you know I want to be with you, so why say that?'

'It's just that being here all alone makes me think...'

'What?'

'That I want to be a family. I want to be happy, and I know I'm not happy here. It's just I've grown used to being here and I'm terrified of doing something that will hurt Jamie and destroy our relationship.'

His voice softens. 'Don't worry Beth, I'll be back soon,'

I wish he was here close to me, but he's far away in some nasty, dangerous country, risking life and limb.

'Come back, say you've had enough and want to return to Athens or London.'

He laughs. 'I can't just end it like that. You should know that. I have a contract.'

'Yes, well, do what you can to end it and come back here as quickly as you can. You don't have to spend the rest of your time there. Just say you want out. Finish the time you must work for them either here in London or in Athens, then we'll stay in Cornwall for a few weeks and see what we all think of it.'

'I must go now. Take care, Beth, and call me if you need anything.'

'I always do, don't I?'

'Bye, Beth.'

The phone clicks and he's gone, and I'm left sitting wondering which awful country he's in right now.

12
___

NEWSROOM

His phone rings. Still staring at the screen in front of him he absentmindedly grabs it.

'Yes?'

'Is that Fred, son of Elouise?'

'Yes.'

'I'm calling about your mother, Fred.'

'Who is that?'

'The Nice hospital. She had a fall — she's okay but wants to leave the hospital. She's very strong-willed but we don't think it's good for her to go, not yet. Is it possible for you to come and see her?'

'Yes, tell her to do nothing till I get there.'

He sits staring at his phone, muttering to himself. I must get Sofia to help Beth. We need to get this story, and she's the only one who can really help, but I must be there when they meet, otherwise Beth won't bother seeing her again. She'll stick with Stuart. She'll get more from working with Sofia, but only if they get on. I must make sure they get off to a good start together otherwise...

'Hi Sofia, it's Fred. Is it possible for us to meet for a quick drink I need...'

'I'm busy Fred—maybe tomorrow.'

'It must be now; I've got to go to France — my mother's ill. I wondered if you could help because the story we're covering is in Hampstead, where you're based now.'

'I'm sorry about your mum, but I'm really busy can't you get Stuart Johnson to help?'

'We talked about it with him, but he's even more difficult to get hold of than you. I wouldn't ask if it wasn't so important.'

'Is there something you're not telling me, Fred?'

'I'd like you to meet Beth, who's working with me.'

Silence.

'I thought it would be a good idea if she comes with me. It'll give you the chance to get to know each other...'

'Okay, but just ten minutes.'

'Great. Where are you?'

'At the station.'

'Good, can we meet in that cafe or the pub around the corner? They're close to you?'

'Okay. I'm on a case now, so I'll have to slip out. I'm already in their black books, so I don't want to shake the boat any more than I have to. We must make it short — fifteen minutes maximum, then I leave.'

She hangs up.

Fred knows what she's like—she's an excellent detective but often very strong minded, which doesn't seem to go down well with some people.

He hits Beth's number.

It goes to voicemail.

Where the hell is she?

He tries her home number.

Her mum answers.

'Is Beth there?'

'Yes, she's on the phone.'

'Please tell her it's urgent. I must speak to her.'

'Something wrong, Fred?'

'Yes, my mum's in hospital. I need to see her.'

'I'm so sorry to hear that, Fred. Hold on, I'll get her for you.'

A minute later Beth's on the phone.

'Fred, what's happened?'

'Mum's in hospital.'

'Is it bad?'

'They say she's over the worst. She's getting better, but she wants to leave, and they say she shouldn't, not yet anyway.'

'I'll book you a flight and drive you to the airport.'

'No, don't worry about that. There are important things we need to discuss about the story we're covering.'

'Yes, I know, Fred, but I'm quite capable…'

'Meet me at that café in Hampstead, the one near the pub we were at the other morning with Stuart Johnson.'

'Why?'

'Sofia Larson, the one who's filling in for Dawn Dawson while she's on leave in Newcastle, she'll be there. You need to meet. She's a bit curt sometimes, but she's a good detective and she can help you a lot with the Hampstead Tube story. Beth, I'd like you two to get to know each other. Please, for me?'

'But what about Stuart! That's why we went to see him the other morning? '

'Yeah, but you know what he's like. He's difficult to reach, whereas with Sofia she'll help. She's a bit of a toughie, but once you get to know her. We need to get stuff on this Tube murder quickly so we can find out what's happening at the fish market.'

'I'm sorry Fred, it's just that I know Stuart and think he's the best one to work with.'

Suddenly, the door opens and Hardcastle walks into the newsroom.

Fred walks over to the window and whispers in the phone. 'Don't you remember from experience who helped you the most, and it wasn't Stuart, was it? It was DCI Dawn Dawson who Sofia has taken over from. She acts as if she knows everything—and usually does — she's good, Beth. Would I recommend her if I didn't have faith in her?'

'Fred, I'd like to meet her, but if she's such a hard person to...'

'Beth, she's like this because someone killed her husband. She has a child, she's a hard worker.'

'When she's at work, who looks after her child?'

'He's on a school break with her mum, but usually the woman next door looks after him when she's at work.'

'I don't know...'

'Be there in twenty minutes?'

'Okay.'

Fred runs over to his desk, grabs his laptop; a few papers, then turns to see Hardcastle glaring at him.

'And where are you going, Fred?'

'Out.'

Hardcastle's eyebrows shoot up. 'And where...?'

Fred ignores him and runs to the door, opens it, and jumps into the stationary elevator.

Outside, he hails down a passing cab.

'Hampstead police station and make it quick, please.'

13

SOFIA LARSON
Café in North London

Twenty minutes later, I'm outside the café.

Where the hell is Fred?

A woman opens the café door to go inside, then turns and looks at me.

I eye her dishevelled appearance — she looks like she's having a bad day like me. I go to look away, then look at her again. Longish brown hair with blond streaks — but it's her face I'm drawn to—it's Sofia, Sofia Larson.

She walks over. 'Beth, it is Beth, isn't it?'

I nod.

'We met before briefly. You were with Fred in Piccadilly Tube. I was in a hurry...'

I walk over to her. 'Yes, we did.' Without realizing it, I'm looking at her hair. She pushes it back from her face and smiles. 'It's grown a bit since I saw you.'

'Yes, and you changed the color.'

'No, I'm naturally brown. The streaks are from the sun.'

With that, she walks into the café, spies a vacant table in the corner near the counter, and sits down. I sit in the chair opposite.

A voice from the counter bellows, 'Yes ladies, what can I get you?'

'*Café cortado* for me,' I say, then catch Sofia watching me.

She takes out her phone from her bag. 'Espresso for me.'

Then the café door bursts open and in walks Fred.

'Sorry I'm a bit late, traffic's bad. Have you ordered?'

The guy behind the counter leans over. 'Yes, they have. Now what can I get you?'

'A large black coffee and a toasted bacon sandwich.'

Sofia turns her gaze from Fred to me. 'How long have you been a reporter?'

'Oh, quite some time now.'

'Always in London?'

'No, I started in Athens after leaving university.'

'As a reporter?'

'Yes.'

'Your coffees ladies.'

He plonks them on the table in front of us, then puts a large mug of black coffee in front of Fred.

'Your sandwich won't be long.'

He walks back to the counter.

Fred grabs his coffee.

Sofia carries on talking. 'Why did you come to London, Beth?'

Taken aback a little by her directness, I just sit looking at my coffee.

Fred's eyes are on me, then on Sofia.

'Better prospects working here?' she says, studying my face, then smiles.

I'm about to ask her how long she's worked for the police when she turns to Fred, who's flicking through his phone.

'You're both covering the case of the woman killed on the Tube?'

He nods, then looks uncertainly from me to Sofia. 'Beth's checking out the husband but as I'll be in France for a few days, she'll be covering both.'

Sofia just sits looking at him, then turns to me. 'Okay, well, if Beth gets to learn anything of interest, I'm sure we can work together.'

'Actually, I was thinking...'

Her shrewd blue eyes are on my face...

'What?'

'I think she was getting information for someone, and she was getting in too deep. It happens a lot when there's big money to be made.'

'What makes you think that?'

I'm about to say, well, it's not rocket science, but don't.

'The cleaner sees her with a USB frequently, syphoning of information from her boss's laptop.'

'Yes, but maybe her boss had asked her to do it?'

I shrug. 'Could be, but why not do it during work time? We need to know what she downloaded and if she gave it to anyone.'

Fred flexes his wrists and gives me a wink. 'When I get back from France...'

She looks at Fred. 'Can you leave going to France for a couple of days?'

He frowns. 'Why?'

Her blue eyes watch him over the rim of the small cup of espresso coffee.

Then, placing it back on the saucer, she stands up. 'I won't be here for a day or two, so it's best you stay here with Beth and go to France when I return.'

His eyebrows shoot up. 'But the hospital said they think I should go now.'

'Is she very ill?'

'She had a fall.'

'So, it's not critical?'

'Well, no, but she wants to leave the hospital. The doctors want her to stay a little longer so they can do more tests.'

'Okay, Fred, this is what you do. Call your mum now and tell her you're coming to the hospital the day after tomorrow. If she says she wants to leave now say well if that's the case, I won't come. I think she'll stay in the hospital.'

Fred looks a little taken aback. 'Okay, I'll call her after I've eaten this.'

'Now Fred, I'm in a hurry.'

Putting down his sandwich, he gets up and walks towards the door, opens it, and goes outside.

Sofia sits flicking through her phone.

Two minutes later, Fred returns and grins at Sofia. 'You were right, she said she'll stay in hospital if I promise to tell the doctors that she's okay to leave when I get there.'

Sofia stands up and looks at him. 'Good, now eat your sandwich.'

Then to me she adds. 'Keep in touch.'

After she's gone, I sit watching Fred munching his sandwich amazed he allows her to boss him around like that.

He wipes his mouth with a serviette, sighs contentedly, then gives me a knowing look.

'I said she rubs people up the wrong way, didn't I?'

'Yes, but...'

'Finish your coffee Beth, we've work to do back at the newsroom.'

14

CANARY WHARF

ON THE TUBE, I check the notes I made when we met Stuart.

He said Orario Odin, the cleaner, when interviewed said the dead woman recently started staying late.

One evening, she saw Julia Ballantyne-Smythe on one of the boss's laptops. She shoved something into the laptop, then after a few minutes, took it out. She did it again in another room. So, from this it looks like Julia was copying files onto a USB.

The cleaner's evidence is only circumstantial, based on what she said. It sounds convincing — the woman working late hadn't done it before.

But then the rest of the staff working there didn't mention this. But they wouldn't, would they? They all have their jobs to think of.

So, it's only the cleaner who saw this happen. Everyone

leaves the offices at 5.00 latest 6.00. Then later in the evening the cleaner comes, so this is what I must find out...
Why did Julia do it?
Was she working with someone or doing it alone?
Was she killed because of this?

I WANT to catch the cleaner or anyone who worked with Julia, so I arrive early at Canary Wharf. It's just coming up to 6.15am when I leave the Tube, yet the place is full of people.

Normally cleaners work either late at night or early in the morning. Whatever hours that fit in with the business.

Stuart's already told us what the cleaner said. I now need to chat with one of her workmates. Everything starts early in the city. The company canteens provide excellent breakfasts and gyms which get the workers in early, keeps them fit for work. It's a win win situation as many of the workers are keen to use the gym before starting work.

As I leave the Tube station, I'm impressed by the area. It's not very busy at the moment, just a few keen workers heading for the gym or canteen. I look for a cafe with a view of the entrance to the building. There's one directly opposite which suits me fine.

Finish coffee, go outside and wait near the building's entrance.

Most of the staff are in a rush and don't have time to look at me, let alone talk. But then a guy in a classic, well-fitted light gray suit makes eye contact with me. He hesitates, then walks over. 'You look a bit lost. Can I be of help?'

He's around mid-30s with reddish brown hair and looks as if he had a late night—reddish eyes either from too much booze or lack of sleep—strange he should stop, although in my business maybe not so strange. It's a good way to pick someone up. Or maybe he's just a nice guy. Hopefully, the latter.

I can tell from his dress he's not short of money. Who is if they work in Canary Wharf? His suit probably costs anything from £1,000 upwards.

'I need to talk to someone about Julia. This is where she worked, isn't it?'

A look of surprise quickly followed with a, 'Oh, sorry, I didn't know her.'

He goes to move away, then turns and looks at me.

'And you are?'

'I'm a friend.'

A cynical smile comes to his mouth. 'Oh, yeah, of course.'

He nods and walks away.

I curse him.

A woman who was hovering behind him comes over. 'What do you want to know and why?' she asks, giving me the once over.

'I need to know what happened before...'

I stop, she's staring at me.

'You're a reporter, aren't you?'

I nod. 'Yes, and I want to find out who killed her.'

A smile lights her face for a second, then it's gone. 'You're not the only one. The police have been interviewing all of us. They say she might have jumped, but Julia would never do that — someone pushed her.'

I return her gaze. 'Can we go somewhere and talk?'

She looks around, then her eyes come to rest on another building near the one where she works. 'On the lower floor of that building over there is a small cafe. I'll try to slip out and meet you there in half an hour.'

I nod and watch as she disappears into the building. This entire area reeks of money. Everyone's well dressed and there's an air of safety around.

After taking the elevator to the lower floor of the building she mentioned, I'm instantly drawn to the delicious aroma of coffee wafting over to me from a small round stand with coffee machines and trays of croissants, sandwiches and cakes strategically placed next to the coffee machine.

This is the financial hub of London and even in this small oasis of calm, the marketing methods are used to their full advantage.

A couple of men sit hunched over laptops muttering to each other, probably about their latest contract or the stocks and shares where their huge profits come from.

Other than them, the place is empty.

I walk over to the counter where a young woman stands filling trays with more appetizing snacks.

She looks over at me and smiles. 'Can I help you?'

'*Cafe cortado* with soya milk?'

She nods. 'I'll bring it over to you.'

15

CANARY WHARF

I sit near the café flicking through my phone, checking the early morning news to see if there's anything new on the Tube murder.

'Your coffee.'

She places it near my hand and goes to walk away when I see the woman I was talking with earlier approaching my table.

I point to my coffee. 'Would you like a coffee?'

She looks at my *café cortado,* then at the waiting young woman.

'A black coffee and a croissant with almonds, please.'

She looks at my phone, then at me. 'You must give me your assurance that you won't use my name and you won't record this.'

'Of course. I'm Beth, here's my card.'

She nods, takes the card, pulls out a chair opposite me, but doesn't offer her name, just sits looking at my card.

'Coffee and croissant,' the young woman announces, placing a large cup of coffee and delicious looking croissant in front of the redhead.

She nods. 'Thanks.'

After adding sugar, she takes a couple of sips, breaks off a piece of the crispy pastry, pops it into her mouth, chews it, then looks at me. 'You think someone killed her, don't you?'

'Yes, and if you can help...'

'What do you want to know?'

'Was she doing anything out of the ordinary lately?'

There's a hint of a smile on her face, then it's gone.

'If you mean was she staying late then, yes she was, and before you ask, I know what that cleaner told the police. Word gets around in here quickly.'

Taking a sip of coffee, she peers at me over the rim. 'You want confirmation of this, don't you?'

I nod.

'I was her friend. We worked together. I knew exactly what she was doing, and I think she wanted to stop, but she was being blackmailed.'

'She told you?'

She nods. 'And before you ask any more questions, check out that detective who's always nosing around here.'

I frown. 'Detective from where?'

'North London, that's all I'm going to say.'

'Did she interview you?'

'No, I was off on sick leave, but I was told she's a nutter. She screamed at one man who worked with Julia just because he said he didn't know if she was being blackmailed.'

I sit watching her while she finishes her croissant and I

IN TOO DEEP

believe her. I also think I know the detective she's referring to.

As if reading my mind, she taps her mouth with a serviette, finishes her coffee and gets ready to leave.

'Are you sure you can't tell me her name? It would help me a lot...'

She smiles. 'Just like I said, she's a toughie, and she's based in North London.'

'So why was she here in Canary Wharf?'

She sighs. 'You know where the murder took place, so draw your own conclusions.' She turns to leave and murmurs. 'Thanks for the coffee.'

I watch as she disappears in the crowd of people and sit thinking about Sofia Larson.

My phone vibrates. It's Fred.

'Yes, Fred?'

'The dead woman was being blackmailed. She was having an affair — it's not a secret. Many people knew, except maybe her husband.'

I'm about to say I know when he says...

'She knew her husband was having it off with the *au pair,* so why didn't she tell her husband?'

'Maybe she didn't know he was having an affair. If she did, wouldn't she have left him? Or maybe she knew it would destroy his career and hers, so she just stuck with it. He was getting his, and she was getting her bit on the side.'

'Yes, but why kill her? The next morning she's on the platform as usual waiting for the Tube to go to work. It's packed with people, then suddenly someone pushes her from behind—she falls—the train's coming towards her...'

'Who would do something so dreadful?'

'I don't know, Beth. That's for us to find out.'

LATER THAT DAY I return to Canary Wharf and wait till the redheaded woman I spoke to earlier leaves work.

I spot her immediately. Bright red hair cut into a bob she's hard to miss. As I walk over, she stops then looks as if she's going to bolt over to the other side of the road. Then, with a resigned sigh, she walks over to me.

'Now I know who you are. You're that journalist. I've seen you on the news you're always covering murders...'

I must have looked surprised because she smiles, then her face changes. 'I shouldn't really talk to you, but she was my friend and I want the bastard caught who did this.'

I say nothing, just wait to see what she says. I can tell she's still not sure if she can trust me, but then she blurts out.

'After work one day we were walking to the Tube when I saw this fellow watching her. As soon as she saw him, she mumbled that she'd forgotten something in her desk and went back.'

'To work?'

'Yes. She changed from being happy and chatting about going on holiday to France to someone who looked frightened. It was when she saw him her face dropped.'

It's as if the redhead's re living it again — she sits with a faraway look in her eyes, then her eyes are on me. 'She looked panic stricken.'

'What did he look like?'

She gives a little satisfied laugh. 'I felt something wasn't right, so I took a photo of him. I'll send it to you but don't you dare say you got it from me, otherwise he'll come after me.'

'Of course not.'

IN TOO DEEP

She nods, then disappears.

AFTER WALKING home across the park, I make something to eat.

Then I think about the times I've been with Dev. Some of them were very dangerous, some very happy, but never dull. Being with Dev is never dull.

Elias is worried about Helen, but I know Helen, and if she's fed up, she just shuts up her travel agency and goes somewhere for a couple of days.

I chop onions to make a meal, then get fed up. Much better to bung a pizza in the microwave and pour myself a glass of red wine.

While I'm waiting for the pizza to cook, I sit thinking about Helen. Where would she go? Maybe she has a new boyfriend. She enjoys driving fast. In Greece she drives like a maniac, and in Spain...

I grab my phone.

'Elias, have you checked the hospitals? The last time I was in Athens, Helen met me from the airport in her new car. It's a very fast car. A supped-up version of someone's car she liked when we were in Spain.'

Elias grunts. 'Why? Do you think she's...'

Shit, now I'm really worried.

'No, I'm just trying to think about where she would go.'

'If you think of anything...'

'Yes, I'll call you Elias.'

I sit glugging my wine.

Mum and Jamie are in Greece — maybe I should ask her if she's heard from Helen.

My phone rings. It's Jamie.

'Jamie, how are you?'

'Great Mum, it's lovely here at Nan's. When are you coming?'

'Soon, just have to finish this story we're on, then I'll get the next plane over. Is Nan alright?'

'Yes, she's just taking a shower. She said she'll call you later. So, you'll be here soon, Mum?'

'Yes, I will. Now have a good time, enjoy swimming in that lovely sea.'

'I will, see you soon Mum.'

Another glug of wine, then the ping from the microwave tells me the pizza's ready.

16

NEXT DAY

I'M in the kitchen making coffee when my phone rings. It's an Athens number, it's Elias.'

'Yes Elias?'

'Beth, this will come as a shock, but I think you should know.'

'What's happened?'

'It's Helen. She had an accident.'

A shiver runs down my spine. 'She's in a hospital in Athens?'

'No, she was driving down that mountain road in Spain, and...'

His voice breaks...

'What Elias?'

'I'm so sorry, Beth, but she's gone.'

'Gone? What do you mean, gone?'

'She's dead Beth.'

My head's spinning.

'David's arranging for her to be flown back to Athens today.'

Silence.

'Beth,' he sobs. 'Book a flight to Athens now. Then call me and let me know when you're arriving. I'll be waiting for you at the airport.'

I drop the phone.

No, it can't be, not Helen, not Helen.

THERE's a knock on the door, then again.

'Beth, open the door.'

I can't move.

'Open the door Beth, it's Fred.'

Dragging myself off the sofa, I open it.

Fred comes in and stands staring at me.

'I'm so sorry I called your mum because I couldn't get hold of you. I didn't know what was wrong.'

I look at him, then turn and stagger back to the sofa. Pick up the bottle of brandy and take another swig.

He stands staring at me; I pass him the bottle. 'Want some?'

He goes to grab the bottle from me. I take it back.

'It looks like you've had enough, Beth. Give me the bottle.'

'I haven't had nearly enough. Why are you here?'

'Come on, Beth, drinking won't help. Give me the bottle...'

'She was my best friend. My only friend. I lost touch with the people I knew from university, and Helen was my only real friend. She knew me and I knew her. We were at school together for two years when I was in Oxford. Well, not in Oxford. The school was in that village. Then she came to Athens...'

I try to get up but fall back on the sofa.

'And now she's gone. Why do they all die?'

'Beth, it's terrible, but...'

'First, it was James, then Nick. Nick, they killed him, and they killed James. And now, they killed Helen. Elias said she had an accident, but I don't believe it.'

Fred stands staring at me, then comes over and hugs me. 'It was an accident. She loved to drive fast, you said so yourself.'

'That's what Elias said, but she knew the roads very well. She was an excellent driver. Somebody killed her. Just like they tried to kill me. There are many of them still out there that should be in prison, but they never caught all of them. That evil kingpins in jail but his people are roaming the streets freely, killing at their leisure. They tried to kill her before and failed and now...'

'Beth...'

'They got her, Fred. They killed her, she's dead.'

'I'll get you a glass of water and make some coffee. It will help.'

I turn round and trip over.

Fred grabs me and holds me tight. 'Beth, I'm so sorry. I don't know what to say. If I can do anything to help...'

'Nobody can do anything...'

I rush to the sink in the kitchen and vomit.

Fred grabs some kitchen paper, wipes my mouth, then picks me up and carries me to my bedroom.

My eyes are closing. 'Go back Fred, I'm alright, do whatever it is Hardcastle wants you to do.'

I feel Fred cover me with the duvet and watch through

slit eyes as he leaves the bedroom and walks towards the living room.

FRED

A phone rings.
It's his phone.
He grabs it from his pocket and stares at the number.
Hardcastle.
Then he remembers.
He finished the bottle of brandy, then fell asleep in Beth's living room.

A text comes through from Hardcastle.

Where are you?
  H

Ignoring it, he gets up, heads over to the kitchen. Puts on the kettle. Rubs his eyes, splashes his face with water, then makes a couple of coffees and takes one into Beth.

He gently nudges her. 'Wake up. I've made you a coffee.'
She groans.
'I'll make some toast.'
'No, I feel ill.'
Fred looks at her pale face. 'Where do you keep your pills?'
'The drawer in the kitchen.'
A moment later, he returns with a glass of water and a couple of paracetamol.
He props her up in bed. 'Here, take these.'
'Don't worry, I'm okay, you must go — Hardcastle will... '

'Forget Hardcastle. Take these, you'll feel better.'

'In a minute.'

'Okay, I'll be in the living room.'

After taking the pills and drinking the coffee, I stagger into the living room where Fred sits drinking his coffee.

'Fred, I must go to Athens. It'll be tomorrow. Elias is arranging everything with mum.'

'I know your mum called me. She was worried because you didn't answer your phone. Get a few things together, and I'll book you a flight.'

'Helen, could always get me a flight...'

'Do you want me to come with you?'

'No, you get on with the story. I'll be back after the funeral.'

'Stay there for a few days with your mum and Jamie.'

'No, I don't want to its better I work. Being in Athens would only make it worse. Just a few weeks ago, it was Alex, and now Helen.'

'I know Beth and I'm deeply sorry, but now you must get ready. I'll book you a flight and take you to the airport.'

'You don't drive.'

'I'll get a cab. Now, have a shower. I'll look for a flight from London City Airport. I think that's quicker than going to Heathrow, don't you?'

'They don't fly direct, book me one leaving from Heathrow.'

17

HELEN'S FUNERAL

FRED DROPS me off at the airport. I go through customs, then onto the plane.

Mum's there to meet me with Elias.

For some reason, it makes me think of the day Elias took Helen and me to the hospital to see James, but we didn't get there in time. I still can't believe Helen's gone. She was so full of life; she had so much to live for...

Mum's running towards me. Her eyes full of tears. Then her arms are around me, holding me tight. Elias puts his arms around both of us. Nothing is said, no words can express the grief we feel.

Elias drops us at Mum's place in Kalamaki, Jamie knows what's happened and as soon as we enter the house he runs over and hugs me.

Although I have no appetite we go onto the veranda and eat one of Mum's homemade dishes she cooked last night.

An array of roasted Mediterranean vegetables, cooked in olive oil sprinkled with garlic, oregano, and lots of black Kalamata olives, which I would normally love, but not now.

After a couple of mouthfuls and a glass of red wine, I head for my bedroom. Mum's place has three bedrooms, so we each have our own room.

The following day, we're at the church, the same church where I was just a few weeks ago, saying goodbye to my ex-Alex, and now I'm saying goodbye to my best friend Helen.

White casket covered with white daisies and lilies, the flowers she loved, are in the front, under the cross.

The scent of the flowers and the heavy scent of incense from that incense holder the priest swings around only adds to my pain.

Helen left no instructions on what to do if this should happen — so she was buried next to her friend James. He was killed, here in Athens, just a year ago. They were very close, and I thought it only befitting they should be next to each other now.

I have lived through many traumatic and exceedingly sad days, but none so painful as this. After the burial, we return to Kalamaki, where Mum has a selection of snacks, drinks, tea, and coffee.

A few of Helen's friends she knew, including Tula, who often helped in her travel agency, are here.

Helen's close friend David and his sister Christina from Spain are also here. It was their hotel Helen was staying at before she took her last drive along that mountain road. As far as we know they were the last people she saw before she left for Granada. She was an excellent driver, a powerful driver, so I find it very hard to believe her car skidded and went over that treacherous mountain road.

After an hour, people start to leave.

David and Christina come over to where I'm standing. Her eyes are full of tears. Putting her arms around me, she holds me close and whispers. 'We share your grief Beth, please come and see us in Spain soon.'

'Yes, of course I will.'

I glance over at David, whose eyes are full of sorrow and a glint of that anger I've often seen before.

'Yes, let me know when you're coming. I'll pick you up from the airport.' He leans forward, and lowering his voice, murmurs. 'I tried calling Dev, but there's no answer. Have you spoken to him recently?'

'No, I tried, but it goes to voicemail.'

He kisses me on the cheeks, then whispers. 'I'll call you.'

After they've gone, I go to my room clutching a large glass of brandy. In some of our darkest times, Helen and I would sit together drinking brandy, and as I take a big glug of the burning amber liquid somehow, it makes me feel as if I'm with her again.

TWO HOURS LATER, I'm with Elias driving to the airport. We have spoken very little, but now he turns to me and murmurs. 'All of us will miss her.' A tear runs down his cheek. He brushes it away. 'She loved life and was just at the beginning of a new adventure.' His voice breaks. A sob comes from deep within him. 'It's so sad, but we must remember the good times we had.'

Placing his hand on mine, he squeezes it, then stops the car outside airport departures.

Without looking at him, I say. 'Do you think it was an accident?'

He sits staring at the wheel for a few seconds, then turns and gives me a worried look. 'Do nothing hasty, Beth. I've been trying to contact Dev, as this is an area he knows about. Human trafficking, and drug smuggling...' He shakes his head. 'But you know all about that, of course, don't you?'

'I asked David what he thought. He said the police say it was an accident, but...'

'What?'

'I don't know if you know this Elias, but he was very close to Helen. He had hoped they might...'

'I didn't know,' mutters Elias. 'What does he think?'

'One of his close friends is a detective. I met him when I was there with Helen. I want to talk to him.'

'Beth, do nothing yet. Do not go to Spain. Wait till I've spoken to Dev.' As if to himself, he groans. 'It's difficult to get hold of him, but I'll keep trying.'

I sit watching him, thinking about the last time I was here in Athens. Without him and Helen, I don't know how we would have managed to...

'Beth, we must go now.'

He goes to open his door.

'No, Elias. I'm sorry, but I want no more goodbyes today.'

Leaning over, I kiss him on the cheek. 'See you soon Elias.'

18

BAYSWATER

I LAY there thinking of Helen but try as I might sleep evades me.

A floorboard creaks outside my bedroom door.

I sit up in bed.

Am I imagining it?

I should get up...

I lay propped up on my arm for a few minutes and all is quiet. I hate these old Victorian buildings. They may look nice from the outside, but they need to be gutted and redone inside.

Whatever it was I heard was probably something I hate. Things crawling around in the walls. I shudder and try not to think of them. At least in Greece, the houses have floors made of marble and thick stone walls. Nothing can get through that.

Feeling a little reassured, I lay back on the bed. If I get up now, I'll only have another drink to calm my nerves, and

I've had enough already. Mum has some Valium in her drawer — she told me to take one if I felt it was all too much.

I lay there thinking of Mum and Jamie. My eyes close, then suddenly I'm wide awake.

A man's looking at me.

A feeling of rage sweeps through me as he comes closer with what looks like a cloth in his hand.

Even from here I can smell it — it's that smell again — chloroform. He wants to drug me.

'Get out of here,' I yell, sliding out of the bed on the furthest side away from him.

He looks strong. He's wearing a balaclava.

Suddenly, he almost pounces on me.

He grabs my wrist with one hand and hauls me across the bed — all the time trying to cover my face with that piece of cloth.

I try kicking him in the balls, but I can't reach.

He laughs, mutters something I don't understand, then he's trying to pull off my nightie.

In desperation, I try to gain some leverage by placing my other foot on the bed, then with all my strength I try to kick him, but he turns. I miss him. I can't move. His breathing's heavy. I must do something before he...

He raises himself.

Now's my chance.

A kick to his groin.

He screams but he's strong, and if I don't do something quickly...

Grabbing the marble table lamp next to my bed, I smash it over his head.

He falls off the bed. He's on his knees, blood streaming down his face.

He tries to make a grab for my leg.

I hit him again.

He sinks to the floor.

Shaking with fury, I grab my phone and call Dev. It goes to voicemail. I call the police.

'A man tried to kill me. Get here quickly before he wakes up.'

I grab my dressing gown from the chair, slip into it and stand over him, holding the marble table lamp ready to hit him again.

TEN MINUTES LATER, the police are at my apartment.

I tell them what happened and watch as they cuff him and take off the balaclava.

His dark hair's plastered to his head. Evil eyes peer over at me. He mutters something under his breath, then he's dragged from my room and into a waiting police van.

After giving my statement to the police, they leave.

With a throbbing head, I run into the bathroom and vomit, then I'm in the kitchen hanging onto the edge of the kitchen sink. I feel like I'm sinking. Tears stream down my face and sobs come from deep down within me.

I hold my head under the tap and let the water run over my head. Then I think of Fred. He wanted to stay — if only I'd let him.

Then I'm in the bathroom under the shower, cleaning every trace of him away.

Was it a random attack or something more sinister? Was he going to kill me?

Not long after, I get a call from another detective who says she wants to have a word with me.

IN TOO DEEP

I don't want to talk to anyone, but when she knocks, I must let her in.

'Did you recognize the man who attacked you?' she asks, taking a seat at the table and pulling out her notepad.

'They already asked me this,' I mutter.

Without looking at me, she says. 'Did you recognize him?'

'No, I've never seen him before.'

'Have you received any threats?'

'No.'

'Is there someone I can call for you?' she asks.

She has a kind face; she reminds me a bit of PC Donnelly.

'No.'

She looks around the living room where Jamie's books are still on the table and photos of him, me and Mum are on the shelf.

'No family?'

'My Mum and son are in Greece.'

'Nobody else I can call to keep you company?'

'No. I'll be okay.'

'Would you like me to make you a cup of tea or something?'

I shake my head — *I just want to be alone.*

She gets up to leave.

'How did he get in?' I ask.

'The balcony door of your kitchen was unlocked. Did you go outside and forget to lock it?'

I nearly say I was drinking so much thinking of Helen, and don't know, but mumble. 'I don't remember.'

She passes me her card. 'If you need me, just call me.'

I nod. 'Do you know who he is?'

She breathes in deeply, eyes me, then shakes her head.

I don't believe her, and she knows it. I can tell by the way she's watching me.

She knows who he is, but just doesn't want to tell me, or can't.

'Have you received the report back from forensics?'

Her eyebrows shoot up. 'Not yet. Now if there's nothing else you can tell me...'

I get up, walk her to the door and watch as she walks towards the elevator, then I close and lock the door.

After making sure all the windows and kitchen door is locked, I crawl into Mum's bed and eventually fall asleep.

19

COACH & HORSES
London

FRED CALLED ME THIS MORNING, but I didn't tell him what happened last night. He'd just come back from a fleeting trip to see his mum and wanted to meet for a chat.

I'm outside the *Coach and Horses*, I give the door a gently push, and then I'm inside the pub.

'Beth, over here ...'

As usual, he's sitting at our table — it's the best table in the pub. It's close to the bar, so easy to get drinks and as most people like to sit by the window, we're normally alone, which is just how we like it.

He sits beaming at me. His light green eyes look greener than usual.

'All is well with mum, I'm so happy,' he murmurs.

Fred really loves his mum and will do anything for her.

Taking off my jacket, I throw it over a chair and sit in the chair next to him.

He passes me a large glass of Sauvignon Blanc. 'Drink this. You look as if you need it.'

Then he looks closer at me. 'What's wrong, Beth?'

I take a large gulp.

He looks at me sharply. 'What happened?'

'I had a visitor last night, but I fought him off.'

His hand flies to his mouth. 'Did the police come?'

I nod, take another gulp of the icy cold liquid.

He sits staring at me.

'How's your mum, Fred?'

'She had a few bumps, but nothing like what happened to you.'

He's staring at the thick make-up I never wear on my face.

'Did he hurt you?'

'A few scratches, but he ended up the worse off.'

'You used your Krav Maga moves on him?'

'He had me on the bed, Fred. I was lucky to get him in the balls, but then he still wouldn't stop, so I smashed my table lamp over his head twice.'

'And that didn't kill him?'

'No.'

'Any idea who he is?'

'Not yet. The police are saying nothing. Can you find out where he's being held and who he is?'

'Of course. Do you think this has anything to do with the story we're covering?'

I shrug.

His face clouds over. 'If you hadn't smashed him over the head with that lamp of yours, things could've been very different.'

I nod.

He sits looking at me, drinking his G&T.

I drink my wine.

'So your mum's okay now?'

'Yes. I felt bad as I wasn't there when it happened. I was thinking maybe I'll get a job in Nice, the weather's better than here and I'd be close to mum.'

'Really?'

'Yes, but the thought of leaving you...'

I sit staring at him.

Is he serious?

Then there's that mischievous glint in his eyes. 'We work together, and sometimes it feels we're more like a married couple — well, except for...'

He raises an eyebrow. 'Well, you know what I mean, don't you?'

I just sit sipping my drink watching him.

'I ordered you a vegan pie.'

No way do I feel like eating, but I can see Molly from the bar walking towards us with our food.

'Hi, you two,' she says, giving us a broad smile. 'I have meat pie and mash and vegan pie.'

'Pie and mash for me,' says Fred.

Molly places our food in front of us, then leaves us to it.

Fred grabs his knife and fork, cuts into the hot steaming pie, then shoves a piece onto his fork and pops it in his mouth.

What he just said made me think. It's true, we get on well, never really argue, and he always makes me feel good.

Without looking at me, he mumbles. 'Eat Beth before it gets cold. It will do you good to get something inside you.'

After a small mouthful of the vegan pie, I take a large swig of the Sauvignon Blanc.

'Any news?' he murmurs.

I look at him and mutter. 'Tube or fish market?'

In a low voice, he mutters. 'I've checked all the news outlets and there's nothing on the fish market murder. Of course, I have friends...'

He has many contacts who always come through when he needs them. 'Yes, I know and if anyone can find out, it's you.'

'Nothing for certain, but I'm getting there. All in good time, Beth.'

The pub door suddenly swings open and in walks DI Sofia Larson.

She glances around the pub, then spots us in the alcove and walks over.

'I thought it was just Fred and me today,' she says, giving him a strange look as she pulls up a chair.

Now he really looks surprised. 'Oh no, I arranged to meet Beth, then I thought it would be a good idea if you came along, so I called you.'

She raises an eyebrow. 'And you forgot to tell me?'

Now I really feel like walking out.

I go to raise myself from my chair — I'm standing up.

Fred looks at me, then at her.

'Are you saying if you knew Beth was coming you...'

'Of course not, I just like to know who I'm meeting.'

I can see she's pissed off, but to behave like this. Does she want him all to herself? If she's not okay working with me, then I'm off.

Fred looks at me. 'Another drink, Beth?'

Fred wants us to get on. I can see it in his eyes.

I sigh, and just for him, I sit down.

'No, I still have one.'

Without looking at me, Sofia turns to Fred. 'Now tell me how France was, and how is your mother?'

'Both are good, thank you. Any news on the Tube murder?'

She shrugs, and I can tell she doesn't want to say anything because I'm here.

I stand up to go.

'I must go Fred — I'll see you tomorrow?'

His eyes nearly pop out of his head.

'No, sit down. We have a lot to discuss.'

'No, really...'

'Sit down, Beth.'

Then popping the last piece of pie into his mouth, he mutters. 'We need to talk.'

I sit down.

He looks at Sofia. 'Anything to eat, Sofia? The meat pie, I can assure you, is very good.'

'No, just a lager.'

'Are you sure you don't want to eat?'

She looks at my half-eaten pie, then mutters. 'No thanks.'

Fred's wiping his face with his serviette, all the time watching me. He knows I've had enough of Sofia, but he wants me to stay, so stay I will.

Two minutes later, Sofia's sipping her lager.

'So, any news on the case?' Fred asks.

'I heard something through the grapevine that might be of interest, but—'

She looks around the pub, then drains her glass. 'We meet in the cafe tomorrow in the outside garden. Much better, don't you think?'

We nod.

'Thanks for the drink.'

'My pleasure,' murmurs Fred.

After she's gone Fred shakes his head. 'She's not always like this. I don't know what got into her.'

'I think I do; I think she likes you, Fred.'

He snorts. 'No way, I'm not her type, and she's not mine. You should know that?'

Before I have time to answer, he gets up. 'I'll go back to the newsroom first. You know what Hardcastle's like about us having long boozy lunches together.'

We both laugh. He orders me a coffee, pays the bill, then goes back to the newsroom.

20

NEWSROOM

Fred walks into the newsroom, looks around.

Good, no Hardcastle.

He pulls out his small mini notebook, then feels a nudge in his back.

'And where have you been?'

'What?'

'You heard me.'

'Having lunch. Why?'

'You were in the *Coach and Horses* with Beth, weren't you?'

'So?'

'You're paid to work, not go drinking in pubs!'

By now Fred's pissed off. 'We were having lunch together. We work bloody hard, and you know that.' Then to himself, he mutters — *'but not for much longer if you carry on like this.'*

'What, what was that you said?'

Fred says nothing, just bites down hard on his tongue.

'It has just come to my attention that instead of following up on the story I gave you, you still think you're covering the Billingsgate murder. Now why would you do that?'

Fred's eyes are like slits staring at him. 'It just come to your attention — what do you mean?'

Hardcastle's face is flushed. He stands staring at Fred. It's as if a blood vessel's about to break at the top of his head.

'Don't play the wise guy with me,' he snorts. 'Instead of working on the Hampstead Tube murder, you're both intent on covering the fish market murder story. Why?'

Fred's eyebrows shoot up. 'What makes you say that?'

Hardcastle can hardly contain himself. 'You think I was born yesterday? I've been doing this for years, I know…'

'You said—*it's come to your attention*. How has it?'

'It doesn't bloody matter how.'

Fred smiles wickedly. 'Oh, but it does.'

Before Hardcastle can answer the door opens and in walks Beth.

Hardcastle's facing the door and sees her and quickly snaps. 'So, you and Fred still think you're covering the fish market story?'

Beth looks at Fred. *He wouldn't have told him — what the hell is Hardcastle on about?*

Hardcastle waves to her desk. 'Take a seat. I want to talk to you both.'

Beth sits at her desk next to Fred's and looks at Hardcastle. She's in no mood to take any kind of shit from this idiot who calls himself an editor.

'Why, what's happened?'

'Don't take me for an idiot,' he screams, thumping Fred's

desk and glaring at her. 'I told you to stop covering that story and yet here we are — you're still covering it. How do you think that makes me look?'

They both stare at him blankly.

'You're not on that story — get it?' he roars.

'You never gave us a reason,' Fred murmurs. 'It would be interesting to know why.'

'I don't have to give you a reason. You're off the story and if you carry on like this, you'll be off this newspaper, period.'

He lowers his head. 'I'm warning you.'

Just then, in walks Harold with a sly smile on his face. He's probably been outside the door listening to Hardcastle's tantrum.

Fred leaps up. 'Harold, are you covering the fish market murder? It seems John doesn't think we can do it.'

His face flushes. 'I don't know what you're talking about.'

'Oh, I think you do, Harold. Always creeping around listening at keyholes. It wouldn't surprise me if you weren't in the pub we were at just now, because how this crap came to Hardcastle's attention...'

'Shut it,' bellows John Hardcastle.

By now he's shaking with rage. 'I should suspend both of you, but I need the Hampstead Tube station murder solved, so you're very lucky to be given another chance. Otherwise, it would be curtains for both of you.'

Fred smirks. 'But you still have Harold, and let me see...'

'You two swan around like you know it all, but there are many who can take your place.'

'We're your top reporters and you know it, John, so why not level with us? We level with you, we both work bloody hard for you, we have a right...'

Hardcastle explodes. 'Get out both of you and don't

come back without that bloody story and then, and only then, will I consider not firing you.'

'And you really think we'll deliver when you threaten us like that?' Beth mutters, standing up staring him out. 'I can assure you I'm not, and I repeat not, working for someone who threatens me. We have laws, and we have a union.'

Hardcastle lets out a groan. 'For fuck's sake, all I want is for you two to bring something back on that bloody tube story. Maybe I got a bit excited, but I won't have my authority challenged. Look up your terms of condition for working for this place. I am the editor and you two are working on the crime beat. So, what I say goes.'

With that, he heads for the door, slams it shut and leaving behind him a deafening silence.

Harold looks from Fred to Beth, then slowly follows Hardcastle out of the room.

'Harold,' shouts Fred. 'I want to talk to you.'

But Harold's having none of it. He hurries towards the door, opens it, then turns and shouts. 'I'm covering a story — don't you two have anything better to do than stand gawping at me?'

'What a wanker,' hisses Fred.

21

BETH & FRED
Bayswater

FRED SITS with that look on his face while he's drinking the coffee I just made him.

'Penny for them?' I ask.

He smiles. 'I'm thinking Harold has a listening device under that table in the *Coach & Horses*. He's always lurking around following us, so how else would Hardcastle know what we said? He's his little gopher and sneak. I can't bear to look at him.'

'I agree. No more *Coach & Horses* for us for a while.'

He sits sipping his coffee, then looks at me. 'Have you heard from the police yet?'

'No. Did you find out who he is?'

'No, but I'm going to,' mutters Fred.

I flick through my phone.

Fred's watching me. 'What about her boss? Have you

found out anything about him — like how long he was going with Julia?'

'No.'

'Does his wife know?'

I shrug.

'What's his wife like?'

'I don't know. I've yet to meet her. I tried twice to talk to her but always got the not available from her PA.'

'Any idea what she does?'

'I think it's something to do with fashion, a fashion magazine.' I get up and walk over to the window. 'We really need to speak to both of them, but how?'

'There's always a way, Beth. We know most papers sell well when the front-page stories are to do with adultery and scandalous affairs.'

'Yes, but we don't run stories like that. What about Sofia? Does she know anything?'

He shakes his head. 'If she does, she's not telling me. Hardcastle wants this story bad, so the quicker we get it, the more time we must find out about this fish market murder.'

'I don't think so, Fred. I think he's playing us for fools. We do as he wants, then when he gets the story he suspends us, and you know as well as I do, we can't take a story from another paper we've been working on with us.'

He looks surprised. 'I didn't know that?'

Sometimes I'm not sure if Fred's joking or not.

'It's to do with ethics and integrity. Check on it because I think if we did it we could lose our licenses as journalists.'

Fred's tapping his fingers on the table, then he gets up and walks around our small living room.

'Do you get lonely here without your mum and Jamie?'

How random. He never fails to surprise me.

'Well, they haven't been gone long, and ...'

I stop, think of Helen and get up. 'How about a brandy?'

He knows where the brandy is kept and gets it down for me. 'I'm sorry Beth, sometimes I say the most stupid things.'

'It's not you, it's just this fucked up life we're living in.'

I feel the tears close to my eyes, so turn and go to the kitchen for a couple of glasses.

He pours a good measure into both glasses, then we sit in silence drinking the amber liquid.

After a few minutes, he says. 'Do you have your notes on the people you've spoken to?'

'About the Tube murder?'

He nods.

'I've only spoken to a few, but there's one thing that really sticks out. I don't know if we can trace him, but I have my suspicions.'

He looks at me expectantly.

My phone lights up.

It's a Spanish number.

It's David.

'Yes.'

'Beth, I had a call from Dev. I thought I should let you know.'

A shiver runs down my spine. I feel icy cold. 'About Helen?'

'No. He thinks you're coming to Spain to see where it happened, and he asked me to tell you to stay away. His words were...

...you know what happened the last time.

Beth, he doesn't want it to happen again.'

'But I went to Spain recently and everything was okay.'

'Yes, Beth, but after what happened to Helen?'

'So, you know what happened?'

'No, I'm not saying that. As far as the police are concerned it was an accident.'

'Oh, David, tell me you really believe that?'

He pauses. 'You know how much I liked Helen, and I really don't want that to happen to you.'

I can't help but gasp. 'So, you're saying I should never come to Spain again?'

Fred gently takes my empty glass from me and places it on the table.

'No, of course I'm not saying that, but you know Dev has contacts. There are people who make a lot of money by giving him information.'

'Did Dev tell you where he is?'

'No. I'm sorry, Beth, but I think you should stay away for the moment. If I hear anything I'll call you immediately.'

'Okay, thanks for calling.'

'Take care, Beth.'

'You too, and say hello to Christina and Jose for me. Tell them I'll be there soon.'

He laughs. 'You never give up, do you, Beth?'

'No, never.'

I sit looking at my phone, then at Fred.

He reaches over and hugs me. 'I'm so sorry Beth, I know you're going through a lot at the moment, and trying to focus on these stories must be so difficult.'

He squeezes me tightly, then says. 'Shall I make us a coffee?'

'No, I need to sleep.'

He nods. Kisses me on the head and leaves.

22

THE FOLLOWING MORNING
7.30am

My phone rings. It's Fred.

'How are you today, Beth?'

'Okay, I'm sorry we didn't finish our chat last night.'

'That's why I'm calling. Was it about Duncan Ballantyne-Smythe? The police can't hold him any longer. They can't find the black hoodie they saw the supposed killer wearing in the CCTV footage from the Tube station. It's not in any of the bins or toilets in the area, so they have no reason to detain him any longer.'

'Anyone could have dumped it somewhere or just got into a car and driven away. Maybe Ballantyne-Smythe walks that way to work. I think they're clutching at straws as there is no evidence, just speculation.'

'Yeah, you're right.'

'Where are you, Fred?'

'On my way to the newsroom.'

'Stop off here for a minute, then when you get to the newsroom, tell Hardcastle that I called you, and I'm out covering the story.'

'Right, I'll get an Uber — see you in a minute.'

I've got the coffee ready, even a plate of croissants. Frozen ones, but Fred loves them anyway.

There's a tap at the door. I look through the spyhole. It's Fred.

'I made coffee and croissants you can munch while I tell you what happened.'

He nods. Comes into the living room, perches on a chair at the table, then munches on a croissant and drinks his coffee.

He looks at me over the rim of his cup. 'Okay, what happened?'

'The first person I spoke to from her workplace started off by saying — *'before I tell you anything, I think you should check out that detective who's always nosing around down here.'*

Then she said she's a nutter. She screamed at one man who worked with Julia because she didn't believe him when he said he didn't know if she was being blackmailed.'

He raises an eyebrow. I carry on.

'I asked her for the detective's name, and she said she's from North London, and that's all she's going to say.'

He stops chewing, grins, then finishes his croissant. 'Sound like anyone we know, Beth?'

'Exactly. So, I asked her if she's based in North London — what was she doing in Canary Wharf?'

'And?'

She said, *'You know where the murder took place, so draw your own conclusions.'*

Fred frowns. 'Sorry Beth, but is this what you wanted to tell me?'

'Of course not, there's more.'

'Go on.'

'I knew she must know more, so at five I started watching for her to leave work. At first I thought she was going to make a bolt for it when she saw me, but she didn't. She came over and talked to me.

Now this is the interesting bit.

One day after work, she was walking to the Tube station with Julia. Suddenly Julia froze and seemed to panic. The redhead — the woman I'm talking to — said there was a man looking at her, and as soon as she saw him, Julia muttered something about having to go back to work. She said it was amazing, and that's not all.

Now Fred looks very interested. 'What else?'

'She took a photo of him. She said she felt something wasn't right.'

'She gave it to you?'

'Yes, after I promised not to say I got it from her. She's terrified he'll come after her — she thinks he did it.'

I show him the photo on my phone. 'Is there any way of finding out who he is?'

Fred examines it and frowns. 'It's blurry, and it would be better if it was full face. I'm not sure, Beth.'

'I thought you might say that, so I thought maybe we should check the CCTV around that area of Canary Wharf and see if we can see him on any of the footage.'

Fred shakes his head. 'Come on Beth, you know as well as I do that reporters only get this kind of information from the police. There might be times when well...'

He stops and looks at me. 'This is Canary Wharf Beth, the most secure area in London. Security guards and police with guns patrol it daily. It has the highest surveillance because it's a major financial hub of the city.'

'So, what now?'

'Leave it with me, I'll have a think.'

'We must do something Fred; this could be the murderer. She's happily walking along with her friend one minute, then when she sees this guy, she panics.'

'Show me that photo again.'

I pass him my phone.

He studies it again. 'Send it to me — I'll find out who he is.'

'How?'

He grins and taps his small mini notebook that's always close by. 'Never you fear. Now get down there and see if you can find out anything else to back this up. We need hard evidence, don't we?'

With his mini notebook tucked safely inside his jacket, he heads for the door. 'Call me later. Maybe we can meet up for a drink. You can let me know how you get on.'

I follow him to the door. 'Yes, Fred, and if you find out who the guy is...'

He turns and looks at me with his mischievous green eyes. 'Yes, Beth, I will do my best.'

23

CANARY WHARF

AFTER FRED'S GONE, I quickly get ready. I have work to do.

Ten minutes later I'm on my way to Bayswater Tube station. After waiting five minutes I hear a rumbling sound in the tunnel — then a circle line train appears.

Doors swish open and in I get.

At Baker Street, I change for the Jubilee line, which will take me to Canary Wharf. Now this is a very secure station. There's no way they can push you onto the platform as glass covers the entrance to the oncoming train.

When the train stops, the glass gates open, and in you get. Very secure, just like everything else about the area.

Security guards are always patrolling with guns at the ready, and should you come here by car there's a barrier with security which they raise and let you drive in.

Sometimes they spot check and stop you. They may

even check your boot or do a swab test of your steering wheel. Everything's done in a friendly, but highly secure way.

I'M PERCHED on a stool in a cafe facing the entrance to the building where Julia worked with my *cafe cortado*. I'm early, so got a shot of caffeine to set me up.

With my coffee cup drained to the last tiny drop — they don't give you much here in London. I head over to the entrance.

Amazingly, it's not me approaching someone as usual, but someone tapping me on the shoulder.

I turn and see a woman with curly brown hair standing beside me, but she's not looking at me.

'You're that reporter, aren't you?'

I must've looked surprised because she adds. 'The one who's covering Julia's...'

She stops, tears spring to her eyes, then she turns away murmuring, 'She was my best friend; a very sweet woman and I want to help.'

Suddenly she goes to walk away, but as she does, she presses something into my hand.

It's her card.

Then she's gone.

I'm a little stunned by it all and with a spring in my step, I return to the cafe, purchase another small shot of caffeine, take a seat where nobody's near me and call her.

'I'll be in Waitrose in thirty minutes. Can you meet me at the cheese counter? Then it will look like we're talking about cheese and won't draw attention?'

'Yes, of course.'

The click of her phone and I'm sat there, thinking about the people Julia worked with. They seem willing to help, but they're obviously afraid someone's watching them and fearful of what will happen if anyone finds out they've been talking to me — a reporter who wants to find out the truth.

The redhead was the same. I wonder how many more there will be tapping me on the shoulder.

A guy sits down on the next stool to me, wraps his long legs around it, then takes a sip of his coffee, and starts coughing.

Quick as a flash, I'm off my perch and walking towards Waitrose.

It's very large with lots to choose from. Some years ago, a couple who were on a TV show about Crete worked here for a while. Thinking of Crete, that beautiful island in the sun makes me think of Athens. I miss Jamie and Mum so much, but try not to think about them. We speak most days on the phone, but I know Jamie wants me there in Athens.

After prowling around the store for some time, I finally reach the cheese counter. Two minutes to go. I wonder if she'll come.

I shouldn't have worried, because suddenly a woman's basket full of sandwiches and fruit knocks me gently. It's her, the woman with the brown curly hair, and she's talking to me while looking at the cheeses in front of us.

'She was going out with the boss. I told her to be careful, but she wouldn't listen. She said, what's good for the goose is good for the gander.'

Leaning forward, she looks closely at one cheese and murmurs. 'You know her husband was having it off with the *au pair,* don't you?'

Taking the cheese, she pops it into her basket and carries on talking.

'I knew something wasn't right, as she kept staying late. One day, I went back and saw what she was up to. I waited outside till she came out, then followed her. She sat next to a guy on a bench for a few minutes, then he got up and walked away and she went to the Tube station.'

'Did you see her do it again?' I murmur.

'I saw her do it twice — maybe she did it again, I don't know, but I was worried. I didn't want her to lose her job.'

I lean forward to look at a large piece of Manchego Spanish cheese. 'Didn't you say anything to her?'

She shrugs, sighs, then looks closely at another piece of cheese.

'She wouldn't talk about it. Shut up like a clam and refused to speak to me. Hope you find who did it.'

I'm just about to show her the photo of the man the redhead gave me, but too late. She's walking away.

Once outside the shopping area I call Fred.

It goes to voicemail.

I leave a message:

Fred, I have something to tell you.
  Where can we meet?

Two minutes later, Fred replies:

That pub at the top of Queensway opposite the park. The one you always go to. I can be there at 7 tonight.

I smile. He hasn't forgotten we had a drink there some time ago.

My reply:

> *See you at 7 tonight.*

24

DI SOFIA LARSON
North London

WHAT SHOULD I DO FIRST? *Try contacting Julia Ballantyne-Smythe's sister again or one of her friends.*

My phone vibrates in my pocket.

It's Sofia.

'Beth, can we meet today?'

To say I'm surprised is putting it mildly. After the other day at the *Coach and Horses,* I didn't expect to hear from her again.

'Okay,' I mutter.

'I'm at the police station in north London. It should take you twenty minutes to get here. Can you manage that?'

'Yes, of course,' I snap.

She's put the phone down.

I sit, shaking my head.

Why so abrupt—does she have a chip on her shoulder or something?

Not wanting to be late, I take an Uber cab. I'll put it down to expenses. So many times, I take the Tube when I should get a cab. Mum said I could use her car, but the traffic's so bad here in London it's often quicker to go by train.

It feels strange going to north London police station and not seeing Dawn Dawson. If Sofia has something for me, fine. If not, then I won't bother seeing her anymore. Stuart Johnson may be difficult to get hold of, but at least he's friendly and does help sometimes.

NORTH LONDON POLICE Station

It's the same officer at reception as the last time I was here.

She looks up and smiles. 'Yes, can I help you?'

'Beth Papadakis, I'm here to see Sofia Larson.'

She picks up a phone, mutters something, then turns to me.

'She's in her office waiting for you.'

I'm about to knock on the door when it opens.

'Beth, how nice to see you,' she beams. 'I'm so glad you could make it.'

Closing the door behind me, she points to a chair opposite her desk. 'Please, have a seat.'

I sit in the chair.

'You've been here before, haven't you?'

'Yes, I came to see Dawn about a serial killer case.'

I remember it clearly, Dawn Dawson perched on the end of her desk, mug of coffee in hand.

'And did she help?'

I nod. 'Yes, she helped a lot. She's a good detective — she has a degree in criminology.'

For a change, Sofia's streaked brown hair is in a bunch at the back of her head. Her blue eyes gaze at mine.

'Okay, I will level with you, Beth. I rarely speak to reporters I don't know, but after thinking about what Fred said, I think I can trust you.'

'What did he say?'

'He talked about things that happened in Greece and Spain. I also checked on what you've been doing in London.'

She smiles, then walks over to the coffee machine. 'Would you like a coffee?'

It's still here Dawn's one little luxury her coffee maker.

'Yes, that would be nice. Black, please.'

She pours two coffees, then puts one on the desk in front of me and points to the sugar. 'Sugar's in the box.'

Dawn's little box with the brown sugar cubes. I pop one into my coffee, stir it, then take a sip. It's still the excellent coffee Dawn uses.

We sit sipping our coffee, and I'm still wondering what she wants from me.

Placing her coffee cup on the saucer, she leans forward. 'You've been doing a lot of digging recently down in Canary Wharf, haven't you?'

My hand stops mid-air with my cup in it. Then I nod, finish the coffee slowly, then place the cup on the saucer.

Leaning forward, she murmurs. 'So, what have you got to tell me?'

Now she has taken me by surprise. Pursing my lips, I look at her shrewd blue eyes. *Does she really think I'm going to share all the time and effort it took to get that information from Julia's two friends?*

She leans back and looks at me. 'We agreed to work together on the Tube case. You find something of interest, and you tell me.'

'Yes, but that applies both ways, doesn't it?'

Her face clouds over for a second, then it's gone. 'You've been speaking with people who worked with the dead woman, and I'd like to know what they said.'

Now she really is rubbing me up the wrong way. I lean back and return her gaze. 'Sofia, it works both ways. If I have something to tell you, I want something in return — that's how it works down here.'

Her eyebrows shoot up, she gets up and walks to the door and opens it.

'Thank you for coming. I thought we could work together on this, but it seems we can't.'

I spring to my feet, leg it to the open door and walk through.

Then I turn and look at her. 'Sofia, I don't work with people who demand information from me. The people I work with give it voluntarily, as do I.'

With that, I turn on my heel and walk down the stairs to the entrance of the police station. My chest's thumping — I want to scream, but I just keep on walking to Hampstead Tube station.

My phone rings. I don't even look at it.

I'm on the platform where Julia met her untimely death, but all I can think of is Sofia, and what a waste of time that was.

25

LATER THAT NIGHT

'I THOUGHT a lot about this before calling you, Beth, then decided you needed to know,' Elias murmurs.

I'm in the kitchen, my laptops on the kitchen table. I've been doing some work and now Elias calls me saying this.

A shiver runs down my spine.

'What is it?'

'It's Dev, he's been hurt.'

'How badly?'

'I don't know, I just know…'

'What happened?'

'I don't know just that he's injured.'

'Where is he?'

'He couldn't say. It was a friend of Dev's who contacted me. Say nothing to anyone. It's highly confidential, but I thought you should know.'

'They must know how bad it is, otherwise, they wouldn't say someone's hurt him. Tell me Elias, I want to know.'

'Beth, sometimes it's better you don't know. Now I feel bad for telling you, it's just that...'

'It's bad, isn't it? Tell me?'

He exhales. 'You're sure you want to know?'

'Elias...'

'He was onto something. There'd been a shooting which he went to investigate, and this led to his car being hit by a grenade. He freed himself from the burning wreck of the car and was on his way back when...'

'What?'

'A very vicious militia group who want information about something ambushed him.'

He stops.

'Sorry Beth, that's all I know.'

'That's quite a lot, and for you to know this it means one of Dev's people must have been there to see what happened. Why didn't they help him?'

Silence.

'Why, Elias, tell me?'

'There were too many of them. They would take him as well. He thought it best to find out where they were taking him, so he followed them.'

'And?'

'It's somewhere... he called it like a jungle. He said he doesn't know exactly where, but this militia group is now using Dev as a bargaining tool to get their people released.'

'Will they do this?'

Silence.

'Elias... he puts his life on the line for this bloody lot, so they'd better rescue him, or..'

'What Beth? What can we do? We are just pawns in this terrible life we live in.'

'So, what you're saying is he's expendable?'

'I didn't say that. Please Beth, I know how you feel,' his voice catches and he stops.

'If only I hadn't said...'

'What?'

'Nothing. Are they doing anything this end to help?'

'I don't know.'

'Who can I go to? We need to get him out, Elias.'

He sighs, a deep sad sigh. 'If I knew, I would ask them myself. Now listen, Beth, they may try to rescue him. We don't know what's happening. What I'm telling you is from someone who's there, and he relayed it to his friend, who then told me. It's of the utmost importance you say nothing, as this may jeopardize things for Dev.'

'Call me if you hear anything, right?'

'Yes, I will.'

Dev's never gone missing before. He's always come back from these dangerous missions. I should've called him, but when I did it went to voicemail, and now I don't know where he is, if he's hurt or...

Elias said he doesn't know anymore, or that's what he's telling me. Who do I know in London who can find out where Dev is. Then a text comes through on my phone on the kitchen table.

Where are you?
  I want results by tonight.
  Call me!
  H

I want to scream and throw my phone at the wall, but I don't. I need my phone to contact someone to help Dev.

Think woman, think...

Who do I know who knows about things like this? I need someone I can trust, but who?

There must be someone I know who can help me find where Dev is and who can help get him out...

Hardcastle's got friends in MI5.

Who do I know who works for MI6 other than Dev?

I sit holding my head, thinking.

It must be someone who works for the government in an influential position. Someone who would know about these things, but who? I don't know anyone like that.

I sit flicking through my phone and stop at Fred. He has ways of getting information nobody else can.

They offered him a job working for the government, but then he decided he'd rather put his skills to work on the streets of London reporting crime.

Can he help me find where Dev is?

26

BAYSWATER

I'M SUPPOSED to be covering this Tube story, and all I want to do is help Dev, but I can't because I don't know where he is.

I try Fred's number again.

Same thing it goes to voicemail.

There's no way of even trying to help him. He's in some bloody country far away from here, probably having his guts kicked out of him right now.

Tears stream down my face, I brush them away and reach for the Brandy in the kitchen cupboard, then stop.

Not the best thing to do right now, is it Beth? Pull yourself together get a grip woman. You just have to hope and bloody pray they rescue him before...

I grab the bottle of brandy and fill a tumbler with just a little drop, gulp it down, then throw the glass into the sink and storm out of the apartment.

IN TOO DEEP

I'll go the back way to the park. That way I won't see anyone other than maybe someone walking their dog.

At the end of the street is Bayswater Road and the park. There's a gap in the cars on the road, so I run across, through the large black wrought-iron gates and into the park.

I'm running and running as fast as I can till I get to the pond, then when I can't run anymore I stop and lean over with my hands on my knees — I'm out of breath, I'm not used to this.

I haven't been running for so long — I used to go for a run every morning but haven't even been going to the gym. I'm so unfit and I'm so very lucky I came out on top the other night. If it hadn't been for my Krav Maga training, I probably wouldn't be here now.

After taking a few more deep breaths, I stand up and start walking around the pond. Ducks, geese and swans with their heads held high, then under the water they go in search of something or just to cool off. They glide across the smooth silky water as if they're on a skating rink dancing to Swan Lake.

An elderly man and a child are feeding the ducks nearby. The little boy laughs as the duck comes near him, then a goose comes a bit too close and grabs a piece of bread from his tiny little hand.

I used to bring Jamie here, and he used to do the same thing, but if they tried to bite him, he'd chase them away, which is good. I want him to grow up strong and be able to defend himself, which reminds me, I must get him to have self-defence classes. In the world we're living in at the moment, you need skills to defend yourself or you're leaving yourself wide open to attack from those who want to harm you.

My phone vibrates in my trouser pocket.

Sliding it out, I look at the number. It's Fred.

'Yes?'

'Where are you?'

'Bayswater.'

'I've been doing some tracking on the wife of Julia's boss. She often goes to Harrods for tea and that other place at the end of Knightsbridge—the museum — you know that place where they have a purple dome for a ceiling and some guy playing the piano. Do you know the one I mean?'

'Yes.'

'Go to both places, as she should be there soon for her afternoon tea break. Are you at home?'

'No, I'm in the park.'

'Good, you can easily take a walk over to Knightsbridge. Pop in and see if she's there; then maybe sit at a table next to her. Get talking. You might find some snippet of information from her. We're desperate to get Hardcastle off our backs. Find out if she knows anything — she's the wife of Julia's boss, so she must know something.'

'Fred, if I knew she was there, I would jump in a cab and go there straight away, but... Fred, I need to talk to you.'

'You don't sound yourself, Beth. Is something wrong?' He pauses, then adds. 'Other than what happened the other night.'

I'm just about to tell him, then stop.

'There is something—tell me?'

'I'll tell you later. It's something I need to talk face to face with you about.'

'It's that confidential?'

'Yes.'

Silence.

'Fred, I'm going home to change. If that woman is there,

send me a photo of her — I don't even know what she looks like.'

'Okay, will do. Are you sure you're alright and you're up for this? I could go, but I don't think she'd start chatting to me.'

'She might,' I mumble. 'You're a very good-looking guy, and you know how to get people talking. That's why you're one of the top reporters, so don't put yourself down. You could easily do it. In fact, we could both go together.'

Then I can talk to him about Dev.

'Not a bad idea. I'll be in touch.'

He hangs up.

I pocket my phone, then run home and wait for Fred to call.

27

BETH'S PLACE

I'M SITTING WAITING for Fred to call.

How on earth can he find out if she's there or not? He hasn't got X-ray eyes?

Maybe he was right, maybe I should've just walked across the park and gone to Harrods or the V&A Museum in my cut downs and T-shirt.

Afternoon tea at Harrods or the V&A or any of the places in London is a tradition many enjoy every day if they have the money to do it but it's something I don't want to do especially when I'm so worried about Dev.

Most of the people going to these places have no cares or worries other than which place to have tea for that day. I remember going to the Ritz once for a treat after we'd just got married. Alex hated it.

My phone dings.

Fred sent me a photo of Olivia Marshall, Allen Marshall's wife.

She looks quite attractive — short sharp cut blond hair, blue eyes, very slim, in fact the ideal person to own and front a top fashion magazine. I think she's half French, so probably that's where she gets that sleek, well-groomed look.

I sit looking at her. An attractive woman, a fashion guru. Why would she ever confide in me? What can I do to get her to say what she thinks of her husband? Someone like that keeps personal things like this tight to themselves. She doesn't look the type to open up to just anyone. She has her image to think of. A strong woman like this wouldn't tell just anyone about her husband's affairs.

It's strange, but you wouldn't think anyone would be unfaithful to her. She's very attractive and seems to be intelligent, but maybe that's what it is. Some men don't like women who are intelligent. They feel threatened — they feel less in control.

Then I think of her husband, who seems to be the complete opposite. He's weak and a womanizer, and although he's good at making money, as far as women are concerned, he's the type who would feel threatened by a strong woman like her.

My phone rings. I ignore it. It's not Fred, it's Sofia Larson.
It rings again.
It's her.
I'm waiting for Fred to call, but it still keeps on ringing.
Eventually I pick it up.
'Sofia, I'm sorry, but I'm expecting a very important phone call. I'll call you...'
She butts in. 'I know you're waiting for Fred to call. I've just been speaking to him.'

'What about?'

'He told me what you two are up to, and I thought I might help.'

'How can you help?' I ask, barely disguising the surprise in my voice.

'Well, not me personally. I have a friend who works at the V&A, the Victoria & Albert Museum. She knows all the people that are regulars in there, so she may be of help to us. If I arrange something with this woman, are you willing to go for afternoon tea?'

'Will you be there as well?'

'I might be in the background somewhere, but I won't be having tea there. You'll be the one having afternoon tea in that beautiful domed room.'

'You've been there before, Sofia?'

'Yes, it's lovely, have you?'

'Yes.'

'Okay, I'll call you back in a minute.'

I sit wondering why Fred didn't call me instead of Sofia, unless…

She said they'd been talking, so if Hardcastle came in Fred would end the call.

Maybe he didn't have time to call me, so he texted Sofia, but why not text me?

Just then, a text comes through from Hardcastle:

I don't know what you two are up to, but I saw Fred texting someone. I asked him what it was about, and he deleted it. Get down here now.

H

I ignore it and sit, waiting for Sofia to call.

Another call comes through.

Why is this happening when I want my line free?

Shit, I really need to talk to Fred.

I'm just about to ignore it, then look again at the number.

It looks like that detective's number.

I check the card she gave me, and it is.

Grabbing my phone before it stops, I answer.

'Yes?'

'Beth, this is Detective O'Hara. I was at your house the other night when the intruder broke in and attacked you. I wonder if you might come to the station now.'

'Now?'

'Yes, if you can. We have something we need to discuss with you.'

'Have you found out the identity of the man who attacked me?'

'As I said, Beth, if you can get down here right away, we can discuss it then.'

'Right, okay, which station is it?'

'Central London Police Station.'

'Oh, where PC Donnelly works?'

She laughs. 'Yes, but PC Donnelly is now a detective, a well-deserved promotion. It's DC Donnelly now, which reminds me. You're a journalist, aren't you, Beth?'

'Yes.'

'On your way over, think of the stories you're working on. Is there someone who might want to harm you?'

'Okay, I'll be there as soon as I can.'

'Good.'

The phone goes dead, and I sit thinking about the Tube story Fred and I are covering.

Who would want to harm me?

28

CENTRAL LONDON POLICE STATION

MAKING sure I've locked everything, and the place is secure before leaving our apartment, I take the back route to Bayswater Road, then cross over into the park. It's much quicker to go this way than taking the bus or getting a cab, plus it gives me time to think.

On my way, I call Sofia Larson.

She picks up immediately.

'Beth.'

'I'm sorry, Sofia, but I can't make it today.'

'Why, what's happened?'

'The police just called. I'm on my way to Central London Police Station to discuss something with them. I don't know how long it will take, so maybe we can do the tea thing tomorrow.'

There's a stunned silence.

'Why are you going to the police station? Did something

happen?'

'Yes, it's about the other night.'

Should I tell her what happened?

She can find out anyway, so it's best she hears it from me first.

'A man broke into my apartment and attacked me.'

'And you fought him off?'

'Yes.'

'So, Fred was right. You are a little fighter. Where were you when he broke in?'

'In bed, trying to sleep. I heard a creak on the floorboard outside my bedroom door, then he was in my room trying to smother my face with a cloth doused in chloroform.'

She sounds surprised, and mutters. 'To be in such a vulnerable position and fight him, you must be trained in self-defence.'

'Yes, I trained in Krav Maga and how to use a gun.'

I can hear the laughter in her voice as she says, 'That's awesome. Of course, I'm sorry it happened, but good for you for getting him. I'll call you tomorrow morning to arrange something for the afternoon. Good luck with the police.'

'Thanks.'

I'm nearing the edge of Hyde Park and cross over to Park Lane. I'm passing the *Coach and Horses* and tempted to pop in to see if Fred's inside, which of course I do. He's not, so I continue my journey to the police station.

WHEN I ARRIVE, I'm taken to Detective O'Hara's room — the door's open, and she waves for me to go inside.

'Thanks for coming, Beth. Take a seat.'

I sit in the chair opposite her.

'Now I already know you're a journalist, so I'll get right to the point.'

I nod.

'What are you covering at the moment?'

I could say the Tube and Billingsgate murders, but just say, 'I'm covering the Hampstead Tube murder.'

She stands up and prowls around the room, looking out of the window, then she's back, sitting behind her desk.

Her long red hair's pulled back into a knot at the back of her head, giving her a slightly severe look, but her twinkling blue eyes and ready smile soften her face.

Leaning forward, arms on her desk, she gazes at me intently. 'Did you think of anyone related to this case who might want to harm you?'

'Not really, but in this job, you can never tell who's watching you, especially at Canary Wharf. All those tall glass buildings where Julia Ballantyne-Smythe worked — who knows who's lurking behind them watching me?'

'Any luck? Did you find out anything?'

'A couple of women who were friends of hers spoke to me.'

She smiles. 'Did they appear nervous talking to you?'

'Of course, but it didn't stop them from approaching me, which is unusual, and took a lot of courage. They're both desperate for the police to find the murderer.'

'Aren't we all?' sighs DI O'Hara. 'So, the person who committed this crime could've seen them talking to you, maybe felt threatened, and...'

'Yes, with all those glass buildings, it would be easy for someone to spot me talking to people who were close to Julia Ballantyne-Smythe.'

'Any ideas, Beth. We need something to go on. I'm sure you know that without me telling you because at the moment we're working in the dark. I need to know if there's a connection between this and the man who attacked you the other night.'

'Don't you know his identity yet?'

She sighs and gives a cynical smile. 'He gave us his name, but we're still checking. He says he's out of work and does the odd job working in catering, driving vans that sort of stuff.'

'So, he gets the money, cash in hand?'

'Yes, but here's the funny thing. When taken into custody he had an awful lot of cash on him. When questioned about it he said he won the money gambling. We're in contact with the immigration authorities to see if they can help.'

She sits flicking through the papers on her desk. I sit thinking. What I find suspicious is if I left the balcony door unlocked. How would he know?

Was it a coincidence that he leapt onto that tiny balcony and broke into my apartment? Or did he have a particular reason for breaking in and attacking me? But why would he want to harm me? Unless… he had a lot of cash on him, so if someone wanted to harm or put me out of action, they could easily get someone like him to do it.

DI O'Hara's watching me closely. 'Have you thought of something, Beth?'

'I was thinking either it was a coincidence, or someone paid him to break in and attack me. You said he had a lot of money on him so...'

She nods. 'Exactly what I was thinking.'

She stands up and walks with me to the door. 'If you think of anything else, you have my card. My priority now is to find out who this young man is and why he attacked you.'

I go to leave the room and she calls out. 'I'll give your regards to DC Donnelly.'

I smile. 'Yes, tell her I'll be in touch.'

She nods and returns to her room.

Once I'm outside, I call Fred. I need to talk to him about Dev.

It goes to voicemail.

I leave a message:

Call me this is urgent!
 Beth

29

LATE AFTERNOON

As I near the park, my phone rings. It's Fred.

I pick up immediately.

'Fred, I...'

'I'm so sorry, Beth. I hope you didn't mind Sofia calling you like that, but none other than the dreaded Hardcastle suddenly interrupted me. I had to text her to get her to call you and...'

'Yes, I know. I thought that's what had happened. Don't worry about that. Sofia and I have spoken about it. I'll be going to the V&A Museum probably tomorrow. She knows someone who works there who might help.'

'That's good. Glad you two are getting on. It's vital in our kind of work to have good connections.'

'Fred, I must talk to you. Can we meet?'

He hesitates.

'This is really, really important; I wouldn't ask you otherwise. It's about Dev.'

'Yes, of course. You're at the park, so that means the *Coach and Horses* must be nearby.'

'Yes, it is.'

'Right, I'll get an Uber and be there in ten minutes. Order me a G&T, and one of those meat pies.'

With a feeling of relief, I walk over to the pub. Order myself a large white wine, Fred's G&T, and meat pie.

Molly's here again today. She smiles. 'Fred really does like these pies, doesn't he?'

'Yes.'

'And a vegan pie for you?' she asks.

'No, nothing for me today, thanks Molly. I'll take the drinks now. Can you bring the pie over when he comes in?'

'Of course, I'll keep it warm for him.'

Our usual table's empty, so I take one next to the window and sit slowly, sipping the icy cold white wine.

I tried calling Elias, but no reply. I left a message for him to call me, but so far he hasn't, which means either he's heard nothing or what he has heard he doesn't want to tell me.

I'm just about to take another sip of wine when the door bursts open and in comes Fred.

'So, what's happening? What's happened to Dev?'

He grabs his G&T and sits looking at me over the rim of the glass while taking a large sip.

'Elias called, it's not good.'

'What happened?'

'A friend of Dev's contacted Elias, and told him...'

Fred's all ears now.

'As you know, these things are highly confidential, so he

didn't tell me much, but I could tell from the way he was talking he might know more than he was telling me.'

Fred nods. 'What did he say?'

Lowering my voice, I lean forward and tell him. 'At first he just said Dev's injured, then eventually he told me more.'

Fred's drinking his G&T, but his eyes never leave my face.

'Dev was onto something which, of course, meant it was dangerous. A grenade hit his car. The car was a wreck, but he got away. On his way back, some militia group ambushed him.'

Fred's eyes are bright. I can tell he's buzzing.

'How can I help?' he asks, then smiles at Molly as she places his pie in front of him.

Molly walks back to the bar.

'Fred, I need to know where he is and what's happening.'

His eyebrows shoot up. 'You mean..?'

'Is a rescue team being sent to get him out?'

'And do you have any idea which part of the globe he's in?'

'All I know is that it's somewhere hot. Elias also mentioned a jungle, but that's all I know.'

'Don't worry, I'll finish this, then do a bit of searching.'

I want to hug him, but I don't.

'I know you have ways and means of doing things, Fred. You're a genius at hacking into things. I just thought you might find out where he is, and...'

'Don't worry, I'll give it my best shot. I'll find out where he is.'

'Elias said this militia group is using him as a bargaining tool to get their people released.'

He nods, wipes his mouth with his serviette, drains his glass and gets ready to leave. 'I know this must've come as an awful shock, Beth, and I quite understand if you don't want to go to the V&A tomorrow.'

'I need to keep busy, and if I know there's some hope of finding him.'

Fred nods. 'Stops you thinking, doesn't it?'

I nod. 'I'll go through the Tube murder notes. I haven't spoken to Julia's sister yet. It's difficult to find a way of talking to any of her family.'

'You've had other things on your mind, Beth.'

I go to say something, and he holds up his hand. 'You're having a hard time now, so don't worry. We've been in worse case scenarios than this before and always pulled it off.'

'I've had some luck with two of her friends in Canary Wharf, but after speaking to Detective O'Hara, I need to think about the guy who attacked me. Was it a random attack or is it connected to the Tube murder case?'

Fred's staring at me.

'That's where I was when I called you.'

His face is deadly serious now. 'Central London Police Station?'

'Yes.'

He gets up. 'I'll need to pop home now as I might need more than just this.' He taps his pocket where his mini notebook is and winks.

'I'll call for an Uber,' I mutter, taking out my phone.

'No, let's go outside and get a cab. I need a bit of fresh air.'

Two minutes later he hails down a passing black taxi and gives my address to the taxi driver, then opens the back door.

'I'll drop you off at your place, then go home where I have all my gadgets to work on this.'

30

NEXT DAY

I'M at home and so far, I've received no phone call or even a text from Sofia Larson. It's getting close to afternoon teatime, so maybe the woman at the V&A can't help, or something important cropped up for Sofia.

While waiting for her I tried to contact Tabitha Jensen, Julia's sister, but I can't get through. Not available. Sorry is all I get. She works in the city, and that's where I'm off to when my phone rings.

'Beth, I'm sorry it took so long. You probably thought I wouldn't call, but I've been waiting and making sure everything will be ready.'

'Ready?'

'Yes, and now it is. There's a reservation for Olivia Marshall for a table for two this afternoon. The table's near the piano.' She pauses, then carries on. 'They have a piano there, but of course, you know that don't you?'

Without waiting for a reply, she continues.

'Go to the table right behind them — my friend will make sure nobody sits there as it will have a reserved card on it. The music from the pianist is so relaxing, which benefits us.'

To say I'm amazed is putting it mildly. 'Sofia, how can she do this?'

'Don't worry about that — all you must do is show up for afternoon tea, which, as you know, is very good. Let me know how it goes — good luck!'

'I really wasn't expecting that. I'm already showered and ready. All I must do is change.'

With my green silky dress and a pair of low heeled dark green shoes, I gaze at myself in the mirror. My hair's grown a lot longer, so I twist it up into a French pleat, don a pair of large glasses and look totally different from how I looked fifteen minutes ago.

All I need now is my jacket. Check I have my phone with me, then I stop. Sofia didn't mention a time.

When am I supposed to be there?

I'm just about to call her when my phone rings.

'Sorry, I forgot to tell you — they're usually there at 4:00 pm. Afternoon tea is around four in England, isn't it?'

'It's 3.30 now, I'd better get a move on.'

'Don't worry, get a cab. You have plenty of time.'

The adrenaline's pumping through me as I run down the steps to the entrance of our block.

Outside I hail down a passing black taxi, open the door and slide into the back seat. 'The V&A. Take the quick route please, I'm in a hurry.'

He grins. 'Victoria and Albert Museum. Jump in love, I know the quick route.'

IN TOO DEEP

Victoria and Albert **Museum**

As I walk into the Victoria and Albert Museum, or V&A as it's known, the splendor of it all hits me. It's so plush and grand, with cafes full of gilded domes, ornate tiles, and walls covered with ceramics. The first time I came here I was so impressed and even now it takes my breath away.

Afternoon tea is a very English thing started by Queen Victoria. Whether it's the full works or just a pot of tea, scones, clotted cream, and jam, it's all very delicious, and considering the surroundings and the piano playing in the background it's an enjoyable way to pass an afternoon in London.

The V&A's original café opened in 1856, then some years later, they demolished it and three separate refreshment rooms, as they're called, built.

For dedicated followers of fashion, the V&A is a dream come true as there are always exhibitions and private shows.

As I near the café, there's the sound of a piano playing.

At the tea counter I stand staring at the cakes, wondering which one to choose — I don't feel like eating, but it must look realistic.

A woman behind the counter gives me a smile. 'Yes, what can I get you?'

'A pot of tea and that cake,' I say, pointing to a small chocolate cake.

Suddenly, a text comes through on my phone.

It's from Sofia.

They're in there. Sit at the table directly behind them. There's a black button on the floor — press it with your foot and you'll be able to hear. It stops when you press it again. They won't be able to hear you, but you can hear them.

After paying, I take the tray with the pot of tea and cake, and head for the tearoom.

I spot them immediately. Walk over to the table behind them with a reserved card on it and yes, there's a small black button underneath it.

As I sit down, I can hear them chattering, but the noise from the room and the piano playing drowns out what they're saying.

Pressing the small button on the floor with my foot, I pour my tea, take a bite of the cake and listen, hoping it all looks very normal to those sitting in the tearoom, but inside my heart's beating fast.

Allen Marshall's wife really looks good. She dresses well and has one of those voices that's easy to listen to. They're talking about fashion, and then the conversation drifts to men. Now I'm listening closely. The woman she's with seems to have a tough time with her husband and thinks he's having an affair.

Then my heart skips a beat. Olivia suddenly says, 'Darling, mine's been having affairs for a long time. He screws anything he can lay his hands on.'

Her friend gives a nervous laugh. 'I don't know why you take it with your looks. You could have anyone you want.'

Olivia doesn't laugh, just sits sipping her tea.

'Who is it now? Do you know which one he's having it off with?'

Olivia pauses. 'Usually, it's a quick fuck, then adios and he moves on to the next one — the last one was a little longer.'

'Do you think he liked her?' her friend asks, while munching on a tiny salmon sandwich.

Olivia sips her tea. 'Maybe she was better in bed than the rest of them, who knows, but it's over now. They all think by dropping their panties for the boss he'll up their salaries, help them climb the ladder to a better position.' She stops and gives a little laugh. 'Allen gets what he wants, then moves on to the next one.'

'So, he dumped her?'

Olivia shrugs.

I nearly choke on my tea as I watch her pour more tea. Her friend's had her fill of the afternoon tea and is now wiping her mouth with a serviette.

Olivia sits sipping tea — no sandwich or cakes for Olivia.

I watch as they finish their tea, then get their things together to leave.

A moment later, they're walking out of the tearoom. I press the button on the floor under the table and sit, finishing my tea and replaying what Olivia had just said in my mind.

Just then, her friend returns to the tearoom.

I turn sideways, pick up my phone and, with head bent, start flicking through my phone.

She bends, picks up a scarf from behind the chair where she was sitting.

Can she see my face? Has she come back deliberately?

Out of the corner of my eye I see her look around, then she throws the scarf around her neck and leaves.

I breathe a sigh of relief.

31

VICTORIA & ALBERT MUSEUM

I'M SO eager to get out of there that I wait just five minutes, then leave a tip for the waitress, then leave the room.

On my way out, I pay a visit to the ladies.

Shock — horror. The two of them are inside washing their hands.

Turning, I rush out into the exhibition hall.

Now I'm outside the museum — I need a cab and fast.

A passing black taxi pulls up beside me. 'Yes, love?'

'Bayswater and take the quickest route — I'm in a hurry.'

The door opens, I slide inside, close the door, and sit thinking. *Has Fred found out where Dev is? Is a rescue team being sent?*

I'm hyped up and full of adrenalin from what just happened, and it's all on tape. With my phone close to my ear, I wait for Fred to pick up.

No reply, he must be busy.

Out of the taxi window I can see the driver's taken the quick route through the park, and we're now turning left into the Bayswater Road.

Ten minutes later, we're drawing up outside my block.

Leaning forward I press a note through the small window into the driver's hand, then get out of the taxi.

He grins, pockets the money, and drives away.

Once inside, my dress and shoes come off.

I'm now wearing a pair of soft cotton beige cut-downs and a short-sleeved top.

In the kitchen, I take a bottle of white wine from the fridge, a large glass from the draining board, fill it to the top and take a gulp of the icy cold liquid.

Then I'm calling Elias.

No reply.

I leave a message.

Call me, Beth

Another gulp of wine.

Shall I try Fred again?

I'm just about to press his number when my phone rings. It's Fred.

'Is everything okay?' he asks.

'Yes. Anything about Dev? Have you found out where he is?'

'Actually, there's something going on in North Africa.'

There's a note of excitement in his voice.

'Is Dev *there*?'

He doesn't reply, just carries on talking.

'I wouldn't say it's a jungle more like dessert with palm trees.' He hesitates, then asks. 'Have you heard from Elias?'

'No, he doesn't pick up. It just goes to voicemail.'

He pauses.

I know Fred — he's thinking about what to say.

'You know something, don't you?'

'I'm not sure, Beth, but it looks like something's happening. I don't want to build up your hopes. Now tell me what happened at the V&A?'

I quickly relate everything that happened.

'Sofia did well,' he mutters. 'I had a feeling she'd come through with something like this.'

'Yes, and I think I know what she'll do next.'

Fred sounds surprised. 'What?'

I sit sipping my wine. 'If she's the detective, I think she is. She'll get her interrogation team into action. And if I'm right Sofia will take the guy who attacked me into an interrogation room, put the pressure on him and tell him exactly what happens to people who kill or attempt to murder someone, and how many years he could go down for.'

Fred stays silent. I carry on.

'From what happened today, I got the feeling something's not right.'

He's silent, waiting for me to tell him more.

I hesitate.

'Come on then, tell me?'

'Olivia Marshall, fashion guru and her mate, were talking about their husband's affairs. A bit on the side didn't seem to bother her, but where Julia was concerned, I got the impression she was glad it was over. She's a very successful woman and has her image to consider, so....'

'So, you think she donned a black hoodie and shoved her under the train?'

'No, I'm not saying that, but then, there's the guy who broke into my apartment.'

He laughs. 'You could be onto something, but there-again, it could've been just a coincidence of him breaking in. He noticed the door was slightly open, and...'

'That's just it, Fred. It wasn't slightly open. I closed it, I just forgot to lock it. We work on the crime beat, so whoever killed her must know a reporter's been talking to Julia's friends.'

'How would they know that?'

'Okay, as an example, let's take Olivia Marshall. She's a very wealthy and influential woman. Her husband's a philanderer, so for her to know who he's going with and for how long the affairs last, she must have spies all over her husband's workplace or cameras planted in there, otherwise how would she know all this?'

He grunts. I carry on. 'A reporter might get a little too close to what really happened, which would fill anyone with fear and fury. Then there's the guy who attacked me. He's desperate to make some quick money, so...'

'Go on?' says Fred.

'I end up dead or temporarily out of action.'

'You could be right, but what about the police? They must be onto it. And what about the guy in that photo you gave me? The one she was seen with in Canary Wharf, the one who seemed to terrify her?'

'When I was with DI O'Hara today at Central London Police Station, she said, they're desperate for any help they can get and to let her know if I think of anything.'

Fred grunts. 'Aren't we all?'

'She also asked if I could think of anyone on the stories that we're covering who might want to harm me.'

'Look Beth, I have a few things to do now. I'll call you back.'

'What are you doing?'

'I can't tell you at the moment. I have to do some searching — you know how I work.'

'Fred, the most important thing right now is to find out where Dev is. Is a rescue team being sent to get him out? That's what I need to know.'

'That's what I'm doing, amongst various other things. Hang in there, Beth. I'll call you soon.'

32

FRED'S PLACE

Fred can barely contain himself from what he's just discovered. A couple of hours searching and now he knows Dev's being held somewhere in what looks like North Africa and hell hole is right. Some of the things he's discovered he won't be telling Beth.

He sits staring at the screen.

Now he's on the edge of his seat. With people like that, Dev doesn't stand a chance.

His fingers fly across his keyboard to unearth more information.

At last, he stops, he goes to his fridge, takes out another coke, then hacks into the forensic report of the guy found in the crate at Billingsgate fish market, and it's just as he thought. Old Hardcastle's being bought — but who's bunging him the money to cover this one up?

By all accounts, this guy was passing information from

his contacts to a minister he worked for in London. He must have crossed or upset them and that's how he ended up in a crate of oysters with a bottle of bolly shoved up his ass.

Fred sits thinking.

If certain sections of the press were to get hold of this information, they'd have a field day, and the government would come under even more scrutiny than they already are.

He sits drinking his coke with his legs up on the desk, reading over his notes with a grim look on his face. He's thinking about tomorrow when he confronts Hardcastle with this.

He's had a good day and is well pleased with himself, but there's one more thing he must do.

An hour later...

Fred's looking at the photo of the guy in Canary Wharf, the one the redhead who worked with Julia Ballantyne-Smythe gave to Beth.

Then he reads through what he's just found out. It appears his name is Jake Ryan — he went to university with Julia and seems to have suddenly come into a lot of money. And from some of the comments on social media platforms, this Jake recently made a killing on the stock market.

He sits drinking his coke.

They're all at it, aren't they?

The lure of big money is too great. Either she was willingly giving him inside information, and they were splitting the proceeds, or he was blackmailing her.

His slender fingers are back on the keyboard, and a few minutes later he leans back and sighs.

Jake Ryan — always in Canary Wharf waiting for Julia. All it took was a couple of minutes for her to pass him the information, then he gets up and leaves.

Now to get this information, she's a willing partner in crime or he has something on her and if made public, it would ruin not only her career, but what about her kids and her husband who's a minister of something in the government?

Suddenly, his computer lights up. He's back on the keyboard.

'Well, I never,' he mutters. 'I must let Beth know.'

33

NEXT DAY
10.30am

I'M in the kitchen waiting for Elias to call when there's a knock on the door, so I check who it is through the spyhole.

It's Fred.

As I open the door Fred comes charging in, and I can tell he's buzzing.

'Fred, what's happened?'

'This is important. I just found out they rescued Dev yesterday and flew him back to the UK.'

I gasp. 'Dev's in London!'

He smiles. 'Well, he's in the UK somewhere.'

'Didn't anyone contact you?' he asks, walking into the living room.

He takes a seat next to the table and pulls out his little mini notebook. I sit down next to him. 'I've heard nothing from anyone about Dev, and I can't get through to Elias.'

His face is inscrutable as he opens his mini notebook.

'What happened, Fred? Is Dev alright?'

His slender fingers are on the keyboard.

'Do you know something? If you do you must tell me?'

He shakes his head. 'Make us a coffee and leave me...'

He stops and looks at me. 'I'm trying to find out, Beth. Make a coffee and if you have any of those croissants—'

He's back on his keyboard.

I sit watching him, then look at the screen.

He frowns. 'I can't work if you watch me, you know that.'

I don't move. I want to see what he's doing — what he's finding out.

He stops. 'Beth...'

It's useless I know the way his mind works — he won't continue with me watching in case he finds something bad.

I get up and walk into the kitchen. Pop two croissants into the microwave, pour two coffees from the pot I made earlier — wait for the microwave to ding, then pop the hot croissants onto a plate.

Fred's hunched-up over his mini notebook when I come into our small living room.

Out of the corner of his eye, he sees me hovering near him and mutters. 'Just leave it on the table.'

I do as he says and return to the kitchen. Sit, sipping my coffee, thinking. While Fred's doing that, I'll call Elias. Maybe this time he'll answer.

Same thing, it goes to voicemail.

I leave a message:

Dev's back in London. Have you spoken to him? Is he alright?

A minute later, a text comes through from Elias.

Don't worry Beth, he's alright.

I text back:

He always calls me. Something's wrong.

His text:

You know who he works for, so be patient. He's okay, and that's the main thing.

'Beth, I've finished,' shouts Fred. 'Sorry, but you know the way I work. It's always better like this.'

'Yes, I know,' I reply, walking over to the table.

His mini notebook's back in his pocket, he's draining the coffee from the cup, and all that's left on the plate are a few crumbs.

'So, did you find anything?'

'Nothing more on Dev, but he's here. He's safe. Don't worry, you know how these things work anyway, don't you?'

'What do you mean?'

He frowns. 'He works for the government, Beth. On no account tell anyone he's back.'

'I just did. I told Elias, and he said as long as he's alright, that's the main thing.'

'Yes, Beth and he's right, isn't he? Now I must be off and do not mention this to anyone else.'

He's walking towards the door. He's in a hurry.

'Where are you going?'

He rolls his eyes. 'I have lots to do, Beth — Dev, the Tube murder, the Billingsgate murder, and then, on top of all this, we have Hardcastle.'

He stops talking and there's that glint of anger in his eyes I've seen so many times before.

'What is it, Fred?'

He looks as if he's about to tell me, then stops.

'Later, when I've sorted it all out.'

'Why not now?'

He gives me a hug. 'Please don't worry, everything's going to be alright.'

He turns to go, then mutters. 'I forgot to tell you. Sofia sent me a text. There's no news about the Tube murder, so…'

'Why didn't she call or text me?'

He shrugs.

'So, I got it wrong?'

He's out of the door, he's walking quickly.

'Call me if you hear anything,' he shouts.

Then he's gone.

34

LATER THAT DAY
The Newsroom...

Hardcastle lays into Fred as soon as he appears in the newsroom.

'So, you've decided to pay us a visit, have you? I've been trying to get hold of you. Where have you been? Holed up in that attic of yours playing with your bloody gadgets. I don't know why you work here.'

Fred says nothing.

This annoys Hardcastle even more.

'I had something — something very important for you, but when I tried to find you, there's no sign of Fred anywhere in the building.'

His face is red with fury as he thumps the desk in front of Fred. 'This is not a nine-to-five job and you bloody-well know that. I really should suspend you and your colleague. I don't know why I keep on giving you two second chances.'

IN TOO DEEP

'Hold on Hardcastle — I wouldn't be so fast in judging people if I were you.'

Hardcastle looks like he's going to hit him.

Fred carries on unconcerned. 'It's come to my attention the body that turned up in that crate in Billingsgate market was the personal assistant of one of the top ministers in government. He's been involved in dubious dealings for some time now. How he ended up in that crate seems to be quite obvious. These criminal gangs don't take too kindly to being crossed, and if anyone upsets them...'

Hardcastle's face is stony, his eyes are like slits.

Fred carries on. He's enjoying it. 'The problem is you've been trying to cover it up, and for who? I would really like to know how much they're paying you to do this?'

By now, Hardcastle looks as if he's about to faint. He passes his hand across his sweating forehead. 'Who told you to poke your nose into this?' he hisses, plucking a handful of tissues from the box on Fred's desk.

He stands mopping the sweat that's dripping down his face. 'You think you're so clever, don't you, Fred? Well, you're not. You're playing with fire and when you play with fire, you get burnt.'

Fred couldn't care less, he's had it up to his neck with the crap Hardcastle dishes out to them.

He looks at him in horror. 'But this is news people should know about.'

'Not when it involves a government minister.'

Fred glares at him. 'All the more reason to publish it. You're in this job to serve the people, not crooks who work for the government. What I'd like to know is how they explained this minister's personal assistant suddenly disappeared?'

Hardcastle gives a deep sigh. 'He wasn't married, so they

said he'd moved to another job in another country — it seemed the best thing to do under the circumstances.'

'And you're going to let them get away with it?'

'Yes, and if you value your job, Fred, you will as well.'

'And if I don't?'

'It's hard to get a job with no references these days.'

'And if I leak it to another paper?'

Hardcastle eyes him angrily. 'I don't think you're that stupid, are you?'

Fred shakes his head. 'You know journalists are a bit like doctors who swear on the Hippocratic Oath to help people. Journalists are there to get the truth and the newspaper must print it, yet you choose to ignore it?'

'Grow up Fred. Don't be such an idealist — this is a jungle and if you want to survive, you must learn when to shut up.'

35

EARLY NEXT MORNING

DEV'S here and he won't, or they won't let him speak to me. The main thing is he's alright.

I sit flicking through my phone, then I see Helen's number and freeze.

Helen...

I should be in Spain. What the hell am I doing sitting here worrying about Tube murders and frozen bodies in crates full of oysters when I should be there, checking to see if it was an accident or not?

I'm checking for flights — there's one leaving in ninety minutes, so if I leave now, I can be back tomorrow, and nobody need know I've gone.

Book the flight, pack a few things in a large shoulder bag, then I'm running down the steps of our apartment block.

I called for an Uber, but they said none were available and I'd have to wait twenty minutes, so I'm walking along

Queensway looking for a cab to take me to Heathrow Airport.

Outside the casino, a black taxi pulls up. A couple of young guys get out and go inside the casino. It's too early for croupiers or punters, so they must work in the restaurant.

I run over to the taxi. 'Heathrow Airport?'

A quick look at my face, then he nods. 'Jump in love, in a hurry, are we?'

'Yes, my plane leaves in just over an hour, so if you could...'

'I'll try my best,' he says, opening the back door for me to get in.

There's a bit of traffic, but other than that, I arrive at the airport with time to spare. If it's quick going through customs, I should be okay.

Sliding out of the taxi, I pay the driver, then head over to departures.

Rows of people lining up to go through customs — will I make it?

With only ten minutes to go, I walk towards the boarding gate, which seems miles away. I run.

Five minutes later, I arrive at the gate.

A young dark-haired guy's looking at me. He looks at my boarding pass and passport and mutters, 'You left it a bit late. I'll let them know you're coming.'

Running down the steps, then through the tunnel, I'm eventually on the plane with my passport and boarding pass still clutched in my hand.

Five minutes later, the plane takes off. I'm in an aisle seat which I prefer and was very lucky to get. The trolley passes me. The hostess smiles.

'Drinks, anyone or something to eat?'

'Yes, a double brandy and a black coffee, please.'

IN TOO DEEP

She passes me two miniature bottles of brandy and a glass. 'Anything to eat?'

'No thanks.'

M*ALAGA* A*IRPORT*, *Spain*

When the plane lands at Malaga Airport, I go straight through customs, then out of arrivals and look for a cab.

Usually, David's here to meet me with his green range rover, but this time I'll get a cab from the taxi rank. He doesn't know I'm coming, and if he did, he'd try to stop me, so why bother?

A few minutes later, I'm in a cab driving along the coastal road, as I've done so many times before inhaling the salty sea air through the open window. I gaze at the sparkling blue sea, then inland at the mountains — all the time thinking of Helen.

An hour later, the cab stops outside the *Hotel Costa Tropical*.

With something akin to a feeling of dread, I climb the few steps into the hotel, then walk over to reception.

Christina's not here, it's Anna, and for some reason I breathe a sigh of relief.

The last time I saw Christina was at Helen's funeral. She said come to Spain soon, and so did David, her brother, but if they knew I was here now, especially after David said Dev had called to tell me not to come here...

Anna looks up, then her eyes open wide. 'Beth, I didn't know you were coming.'

Still looking surprised, she flicks through her computer. 'I don't seem to have a reservation for you, but the room you always stay in is free—the one with the intercommunicating doors, the one...'

She pauses, her face clouds over. 'I'm so sorry, I...'

'Is there another room on a different floor?'

She scrolls through the bookings.

'Yes, on the fourth floor, it's a double room.'

'Good, I'll take it.'

She scrolls to my booking page, hesitates, then passes me a form. 'Just to be sure we have your correct details...'

'But you have this information already?'

She frowns. 'It's a new policy to update any changes there might be such as your telephone number.'

I complete the form, hand it to her, then she gives me the keys.

'Shall I tell Christina you're here?' she asks.

'No, I'll change and come down later when she's here.'

'But she's off today, and David's in Granada till later tonight.'

I can tell she's worried, so give her a quick smile.

She looks relieved. 'He won't be back till late, so...'

'Don't worry Anna, I'll have a quick nap, then get something to eat — take a stroll by the beach, then have an early night. I'll see him tomorrow.'

I walk over to the waiting elevator — hit the button for my floor, the elevator doors close, I take out my phone to call Elias, then stop.

Not a good idea. I have a feeling he knows more than he's telling me about Dev. If I let him know where I am, then he will tell Dev.

36

Hotel Costa Tropical
  Lunchtime...

THE ROOM LOOKS like the one I usually have with rose petals in the shape of a heart on the bed. There's a small fridge and inside is a bottle of white wine, cheese, butter, milk, and a packet of fresh rolls. There's also a small microwave.

Everything's the same except Helen's not here.

If Dev was...

I stop. He mustn't know I'm in Spain. He has enough on his plate right now — recovering from his ordeal. Knowing I'm here would only make it worse for him.

I walk onto the balcony and inhale the familiar scent of flowers and the sea — it all reminds me of being here with Helen.

After a glass of ice-cold white wine, I take a quick shower, change into soft khaki trousers and a top, then call down to reception to send me a pot of coffee and a cheese sandwich.

Five minutes later, there's a tap on the door. It's one of the waiters from the restaurant with my coffee and sandwich.

FIFTEEN MINUTES LATER, I've booked a cab to collect me from the back entrance of the hotel. I'm just about to walk through reception to the back when I see David's detective friend.

His back is towards me. Is he waiting to talk to David about Helen or just here on a curtesy call? Doesn't he know David's in Granada?

Turning, I hurry through the hotel, then out of the back entrance into the garden.

They said the cab would be here in ten minutes, so while I'm waiting, I plan what I'm going to do.

It's now 2.30pm so it will be easy to find the spot where it happened. The last time I spoke with David, he told me where it was. There are many flowers marking the edge of the mountain road where it happened. It's early afternoon so I should be able to find it. I already told the cab company that I wanted the driver to wait, then bring me back to the hotel.

I really need to see the forensic report, but I doubt if the police will show it to me. I'll take photos of the area, and...

Then I think of Fred. If they won't show me the forensic report, I'll get him to hack into it for me.

My phone rings—number unknown.

Maybe it's the cab.

'Yes?'

'Beth!'

I know that voice.

'Beth, it's Miguel.'

Just to hear his voice sends shivers down my spine.

'Listen carefully, Beth. Book a return flight to London as quickly as you can. David can take you to the airport tonight. Do not take a cab, understand?'

Now I am surprised. 'Miguel, why are you saying this?'

He sighs. 'Because it's very dangerous for you to be here now.'

'Is this because of Helen? Do you have proof that it wasn't an accident?'

'Yes.'

'Then why not tell the police?'

'Many of Milos's people are still working for them.'

'Why do you stay here?'

'I'm not in Spain.' He pauses, then asks. 'Are you in your room?'

'No, I'm waiting at the back entrance of the hotel for a cab.'

A sharp intake of breath. 'Go back inside now. I'll call to check you're in your room. Do it now, Beth.'

'Okay, I'll cancel the cab and go to my room,' I mutter, then add. 'How did you know I was here?'

'I have friends, go, go inside quickly.'

Suddenly there's a knife at my throat.

'Walk nice and quiet to that black car or I'll slit your throat.'

He's right behind me, holding the knife at the side of my throat.

Slipping my phone into my trouser pocket, hoping Miguel can hear what's happening, I glance around the garden. At the end of the garden there's a black car, and it's not my cab.

I must do something quickly...

I kick back as hard as I can with my heel, then again and again. He screams with pain. I turn and grab the knife from his hand, and with my arm around his neck, I press the tip of the knife into his neck. 'Walk to the hotel or I'll stick this knife deep inside you.'

He doesn't move. I kick him in the back of the leg.

He falls. A few more kicks, and he's flat out on the ground.

Then out of the corner of my eye I see a man sliding out of the black car — he's coming for me. I turn to run back to the hotel when suddenly the hotel alarm blasts through the hotel gardens.

The man coming towards me stops — security guards with guns held high run into the garden. He turns and tries to leg it back to the waiting black car, which has the back door open, ready for him to jump inside and make their getaway.

The sound of gunshots ring out all around me.

He's on the ground, holding his leg.

More rounds of bullets hit the black car's tires and windows.

A few minutes later, three men lay bleeding at the back entrance of the hotel, hands tied behind their backs.

37

Hotel Costa Tropical
   Late afternoon...

'Another brandy?'

I nod. 'Yes, please.'

Taking my brandy from the bar, I walk over to a table overlooking the sea. I've sat here many times before with Dev, Helen, and David and now I'm sitting here alone drinking the amber liquid we always drink during times like this.

The liquid burns deep inside me, igniting feelings of sorrow and anger — it wasn't an accident Milos's men murdered her. He's in prison, but his evil is still present as he pays men to carry on his work. I remember being on that mountain road with Milos and his men — I was lucky, but Helen...

Another gulp of the fiery amber liquid.

I need to know what happened and if the police won't tell me...

David's on his way back from Granada. His detective friend's still prowling around the garden with the forensic team. Christina came as soon as she knew what had happened and is now in reception with Anna, trying to calm the terrified guests who witnessed or heard the shooting.

My phone lights up — number unknown.

'Yes?'

'Beth, you are not safe. A few of his men are in custody, but many are still involved in drugs and people trafficking. Some of the police are Milos's men. You must leave as soon as David comes back.'

'Miguel, you told someone in the hotel, didn't you? You heard what was happening on my phone — that's why the hotel alarm went off and security guards with guns appeared in the garden.'

He doesn't reply.

'Miguel, I want to know what happened to Helen?'

'And how will that help?' He pauses, then adds. 'I haven't stopped loving you and if you feel anything for me, you must go now. I want to know you are safe. Do this for me.'

He's gone, he's hung up.

The screech of tires — the sound of running feet — then David's standing staring at me. 'I came as soon as I heard.'

He sits next to me and grabs my hands. 'Why didn't you call me? I would have...'

'Told me not to come.'

'Yes, Beth.'

'But in Athens you said come to Spain soon.'

He draws in a deep breath. 'I didn't realize how bad it was here.' His grip on my hands tightens. 'I'm taking you to the airport.'

He stands up. 'Come quickly, do not delay.'

I sit staring at him. Miguel, and now David, wants me out of Spain fast. I know I just had a narrow escape, but...

'They are out there, watching you now, Beth. Milos wants you dead.'

His face is deadly serious. 'Come with me now, we must be quick, it's not safe even in here.'

Together, we walk into the hotel, which is packed with frantic guests desperate to know what's happening. David's face is grim as we walk to the elevator. He hits the call button.

Once inside he murmurs, 'I know you want to know what happened.'

'Yes, I do. You know, don't you, David?'

He swallows, his eyes glint with anger. 'She went to Granada — she had a drink in that hotel she likes, and while she was there, someone cut the brakes on her car. They tried to make it look like an accident.' He looks at me. 'They tried this with you, so you must understand how important it is for you to leave now. You're not safe here at the moment, Beth.'

'How do you know someone cut the brakes?'

'My friend, the detective told me.'

'Was it on the forensics report?'

'He didn't say, just that someone cut the brakes.'

The elevator doors open, we walk towards my room. He takes out his phone and looks at me. 'I'll find out when the next flight is leaving for London — can you pack your things?'

I nod.

Ten minutes later, with my flight leaving in just over an hour, we're driving along the coastal road to Malaga.

We hardly talk on the way to the airport. David's deep in

thought, and all I can think of is that mountain road and Helen.

38

Leaving Malaga
 8.15pm

ON THE FLIGHT BACK, I can't stop thinking about Helen. If only I hadn't been in such a rush — I asked if it was urgent, and she said she'd call me back later. If only she had, maybe she wouldn't have gone to Spain.

David said she was in high spirits, as usual. They'd had dinner on the terrace. She told him she wanted to leave Athens and buy a business in Spain. She always said she'd like to have a small hotel by the sea and because of this bastard, her dreams will never come true.

They say they're putting all their resources into finding these criminals who make so much money from people trafficking, and yet it's still happening, it never stops. You'd think with all the equipment they have at their fingertips, these terrible criminals would all be in jail.

Draining my glass of wine, I look out of the small window beside me at the darkness outside. This will never stop because they must find all the corrupt officials who work in this multi-million business of illegally trafficking people. These people must be held to account for their terrible crimes, but first they must find them.

Back in London

We're one hour behind Spain, so it's nearly eleven in the evening when I arrive back in London.

Outside the airport, I hail down a cab. The roads are empty, so in just over thirty minutes, the cab's drawing up outside my apartment.

Ten minutes later, I'm sprawled out on the sofa with a glass of wine in my hand. The microwave dings — pizza's ready, but now I don't feel hungry.

I'm checking my emails and messages. There's one from Fred to call him. Another from Sofia. Then I see one from Mum to call her. I grab my phone, then stop.

They're two hours ahead in Greece, so it's two in the morning there — I'll call her when I wake up.

I'm just about to fall into bed when a text comes through.

Call me.
   Fred

I would if I could, but I feel tired.
My head hits the pillow. I'll call him in the morning.

IN TOO DEEP

Next morning...

There's the sound of talking — aromas wafting into my room of coffee and toast.

I sit up in bed, grab my phone.

It's 9.45am.

Leaping out of bed, I run into the kitchen.

Mum and Jamie look up.

'I didn't know you were coming...'

Mum smiles, comes over and hugs me. 'We thought we'd surprise you. I called Fred, and he said you'd been very busy, so you were probably sleeping.'

Jamie's arms are around me. 'We missed you, Mum; you didn't come to Greece.'

'I know, and I'm sorry. I wanted to come, but there have been so many things...'

He gives me one of his looks, then grins. 'It's alright Mum, next time we'll go together.'

'Sit down, Beth, have some coffee and eat some of this scrambled tofu. It's vegan, something I found in the supermarket in Queensway.'

'What time did you get here?'

Jamie chirps in. 'We arrived at 7.00 this morning. It was a night flight. I slept on the plane, and so did Nan.'

Mum passes me a large cup of coffee. 'How have you been?'

I sit sipping the coffee, Jamie looks at me, then at Mum. 'Is it alright if I go for a walk in the park?'

I smile and hug him. 'Of course, just don't go too far.'

Two minutes later, it's just Mum and me sitting in the kitchen drinking coffee.

She sits watching me. 'Elias came round last night. It was late when he arrived. We had dinner...'

'Did he know you were getting a night flight to London?'

'Oh, yes. We'd arranged it the day before. He dropped us off at the airport. He's been round to see us almost every day since...'

'You should've texted me, Mum.'

She shrugs. 'I know you're busy. Fred and Elias said you're up to your eyes at work. Why don't you get dressed, then we can go for a quick walk.'

'Are you sure you don't want to sleep?'

'I'll have a nap when we get back.'

She gives me one of her scrutinizing looks. 'You were asleep in my bed. Is something wrong, Beth?'

Oh my god, I'd forgotten about that.

'They were making a lot of noise above my room, so for the past few nights, I've been sleeping there.'

I can tell she doesn't believe me, but she says nothing, just starts placing the breakfast things into the sink.

'I'll have a quick shower, Mum. I won't be long, then we can go to the park.'

'Good, a bit of fresh air will do you good.'

On our walk, we meet Jamie near the pond, feeding the ducks. He always loves doing this. It's a lovely day. The sun's shining, but I can see Mum's tired.

Ten minutes later we're back at home. Jamie disappears into his room and is soon sprawled across his bed, fast asleep. Mum changes into her PJs and is soon asleep.

My phone flashes.

It's a text from Fred.

Where are you?
 We need to talk.
 Fred

39

FRED & BETH

SO AS NOT TO DISTURB THEM, I go onto the small kitchen balcony and call Fred.

'Beth, I was getting worried. You're not answering your calls. I even came round to your place yesterday, and you weren't there, or you didn't answer the door. Is everything alright?'

'Yes, I've just been busy. Mum and Jamie came back this morning.'

'Ah, I didn't know.' He hesitates, then adds. 'So, you've been getting things ready for them?'

Why so many questions?

'Yeah, so what's happening?'

Silence.

'Are you sure everything's alright, Beth?'

'Yes, of course.'

'Did you meet them from the airport?'

'No, I didn't. Why so many questions?'

He grunts. 'I was just worried. You haven't been yourself recently.'

'I'm fine. So, have you any news?'

'Sofia called you, but you didn't reply.'

'Oh, I must've missed it. Why has anything happened?'

'Can we meet at that pub overlooking the park? You're at home, aren't you?'

'Yes. Mum and Jamie are having a nap. They caught a night flight and arrived early this morning.'

'Okay, I'll be there in ten minutes.'

He hangs up.

Pub overlooking the park...

Fred's already there when I reach the pub with his G&T, a packet of crisps, and a white wine for me.

The pub's not very busy. Fred's at a table near the window with a view of the park.

'He looks at his crisps, then at me. Do you want something to eat?'

'No, just one of your crisps will do.'

He grins, passes me the packet, then frowns. 'Are you sure you're okay, Beth?'

'Yes, now tell me the news.'

He takes a large gulp of his G&T, then leans forward. 'That guy, the one who broke into your place and attacked you. Sofia thinks they paid him to do it — you said DI O'Hara said he had a lot of cash on him.'

He grins mischievously, pops a crisp into his mouth, then washes it down with another glug of G&T.

'You'll be getting a call or a text from Sofia soon. I told

her you've been busy so missed her call. We don't want to upset her, do we?'

I take a large gulp of the icy-cold white wine. He finishes his G&T, then goes to the bar for more drinks.

'Nothing for me, Fred. I must stay sober.'

'Ah, yes, of course.'

He returns with another G&T and nearly chokes on his second gulp.

'Eat something Fred. You need more than a packet of crisps to soak that lot up.'

He nods. 'I just ordered one of their pies. Now listen, Beth, this is big.'

He looks so excited, it's as if he's about to burst.

'It seems a personal assistant to one of our ministers in government was passing information from the Middle East to his boss.'

He sits watching me.

'You hacked...'

He nods. 'You should read it, Beth. It's front-page news. *The Billingsgate Murder.* The guy in that crate of oysters at the fish market was the personal assistant.'

'But...'

'It took some time.' He flexes his wrists, then grins. 'The forensic report on the guy in the crate at Billingsgate fish market was just as I thought. I did a little more digging and guess what?'

'What?'

'Hardcastle was covering it up, so I went to the newsroom and told him what I'd found out.'

'And he agreed to print it, just like that?'

'A little persuasion goes a long way, Beth. Plus, I reminded him that his job is to print the truth.'

He sighs and sits looking at me.

'What about your job?'

'I did my job, and he printed it. If they don't like the truth, then I'd rather do something else with my life.'

I'm still stunned — Hardcastle was covering it up, but for who?

Fred smiles. 'It would eventually come out, anyway. It always does, and when the shit hits the fan...'

The guy behind the bar places Fred's pie in front of him, along with a bottle of sparkling water. He downs a glassful, then orders another bottle and another glass.

'Drink some Beth, it's really quite good.'

I sit sipping the water, waiting for him to say something about Dev, but he just sits eating his pie.

Eventually, I can't bear it anymore. 'Have you heard anything about Dev?'

His eyebrows shoot up. 'Hasn't he called you?' Then, lowering his voice, he mutters. 'Be patient. He's alright. Why don't you call Elias? They are mates, aren't they?'

'Yes, I think I'll do that later tonight.'

'Didn't your mum see Elias in Athens?'

'Yes, most days he was round at her place.'

I sit thinking of Helen, then of my trip to Spain.

'What is it, Beth?'

'I went to Spain. I got back late last night. A lot happened, but I was only there for one day.'

He stops eating and stares at me. 'I knew it. I knew something was wrong when I couldn't get hold of you.'

'On no account, must you tell Dev, promise?'

He nods. 'So, what happened?'

I quickly relate what happened in the garden, Miguel calling me, then the man attacking me, and how Miguel raised the alarm and saved me.

'You can't go back there; you know that don't you?'

I nod.

'Did you find out about Helen?'

'It wasn't an accident they cut her brakes.'

He grabs my hands. 'Oh Beth, I'm so sorry.'

I swallow. 'I haven't seen the forensic report, but David said his detective friend said that's what happened. Miguel knew about it when he called me, and he said it wasn't an accident.'

He frowns. 'Does he still live there?'

'No, I don't know where he is, but he's not in Spain.'

'Then how does he know?'

'He's like you, Fred. He has connections.'

40

BETH'S PLACE

BAYSWATER

'Did you go for a walk, Beth?'

'No, I met Fred in the pub for an update on what's been happening.'

'Oh, yes, I saw the paper at the airport. The Billingsgate Murder.'

I walk into the living room.

Mum follows. 'You worked hard on this, didn't you, Beth?'

'If it hadn't been for Fred, the Billingsgate murder would never have hit the press.'

She nods. 'He's a bright one, that's for sure. You two work well together. It's good to have someone you can trust and get on with.'

I hug her.

Then she murmurs. 'Sit down, there's something I must tell you.'

A feeling of dread sweeps over me.

Mum sits on the sofa, I stay standing, waiting for what's coming.

'Helen's lawyer contacted me to go to his office.'

I sink into a chair next to the table. I remember the lawyer she used for things to do with the house, but for her divorce, it was Dev who helped. That's how I met him.

'Beth, she left everything to you, her house in Kolonaki, and everything else except the travel agency which she left to Tula.'

Helen's house. The house she loved and worked so hard to get!

Deep sobs come from within me, shaking my body. I run from the living room to my bedroom.

A little later, there's a tap at my bedroom door.

I try to stop the sobs. I bite my lip, but all I can think of is the last time I stayed at Helen's house.

Dev turned up unexpectedly and asked me to marry him. Helen was so happy; she opened a bottle of champagne.

Another tap.

'Beth, it's Mum, can I come in?'

The door opens, she comes in and holds me in her arms for a long time. 'I didn't want to upset you, but I thought it best to tell you before they let you know.'

'I know, Mum. It's just so awful. I still can't believe she's gone.'

'Do you want to stay in here for a while or shall I make you a cup of tea or a brandy?'

'I'll stay here for a while — I just need some time.'

One last hug, then she's at the door. 'If you need me, just call or text me, okay?'

I nod.

She closes the door gently.

IN TOO DEEP

I lay for a long time thinking of Helen, then eventually close my eyes and sleep.

Later that evening...

I wake up feeling groggy, then it all comes back to me like a bad dream, but it's not a dream — Helen's not here. Someone killed her.

Hauling myself up, I sit on the edge of the bed, listening to the sound of the night. The occasional car in the street, people coming home after work or a night out. Other than that, it's quiet. It must be late. There's no sound of the TV, Mum, or Jamie.

I go to grab my phone from under my pillow, but it's not there — I must have left it in my bag in the living room.

Padding over to the door, I open it quietly — walk into the living room — my bags where I left it on the table and there's a note from Mum.

Elias called. He wants you to call him. If you feel hungry, there's food in the oven.

I'll make a coffee, then check my phone for any missed calls or texts.

In the kitchen, Mum's laid a place for me with a plate and fork. Inside the oven is a tray of *pastichio* — layers of macaroni and soya mince covered with *béchamel* and cheese, something I normally love, but not tonight.

With my mug of coffee, I sit at the kitchen table, flicking through my phone. So many missed calls. Fred, Elias, DI O'Hara, and Sofia, but nothing from Dev.

It's nearly eleven in the evening here, so one in the morning in Athens. It's a bit too late to call Elias, but he works all hours and, knowing him, he'll be out covering another story.

I send him a text:

Sorry I missed your call. I'm up if you want to call me, otherwise I'll call you tomorrow.

Almost immediately, my phone flashes. It's Elias.

'Elias.'

'Beth, how are you?'

'I'm okay. I fell asleep. Mum left a message saying you'd called. Are you still working or in bed?'

'I've just finished covering a demo in Syntagma.' He pauses, then adds. 'I didn't want to tell you, then decided I should?'

A feeling of dread sweeps over me. This is what he said when he called me about Helen.

'What is it?' I ask, my voice barely a whisper.

He catches on immediately. 'It's nothing to worry about. I just thought you should know.'

I say nothing, waiting for what's coming.

'It's Dev.'

'What about him?'

'I spoke to him yesterday. Beth, he's been through a lot, and he's gone somewhere...'

'Where?'

'I think he wants to be alone; he needs time...'

'What happened to him?'

He doesn't reply.

Thoughts of Miguel flash through my head. I remember

what they did when they caught him, but he pulled through and recovered.

'How bad is it?'

'He needs time to recover. I'm sure he'll contact you soon.'

My head's spinning.

Grabbing a bottle of water from the fridge, I take a gulp.

'Are you alright, Beth?'

'No, I'm not alright. I want to know what happened to him.'

'They tortured him, Beth. He needs time to recover — physically and mentally. I know you want to be with him, but...'

'Is he here in London?'

'No, he's far away from London.'

'Where?'

'If I told you, then you'd get in your car or be on the next train to see him, wouldn't you?'

'Is anyone with him?'

'You mean a nurse or a doctor?'

'Yes.'

'Yes, so don't worry, he's in safe hands.'

'He's in England?'

'Yes, Beth. Now I must go. I need to write up this article; it's been a long night.'

'Sorry, Elias, it's just that...'

'I know, I feel the same, but please don't worry. I shouldn't have told you. He made me promise...'

'I just need to know where he is and if he's alright.'

He draws in a deep breath. 'He's had a bad time. I don't think he wants you to see him right now. Go back to bed and sleep. I'll call you if I have any news, okay?'

'Okay.'

He hangs up.

I take down the bottle of *Metaxa* brandy Mum keeps on the kitchen shelf. Pour myself a large shot, gulp it down, then sit thinking of Dev.

41

NEXT MORNING

I'M JUST ABOUT to go into Bayswater Tube station when my phone flashes.

'Fred?'

'What happened to you yesterday?'

'I'll tell you later.'

'It's 10.30 in the morning, Beth.'

'I know,' I snap. 'I overslept.'

Silence.

Now I feel bad. He's probably worried after what I told him yesterday about me going to Spain.

'Was it anything important?'

'It's Hardcastle. Although he's being hailed as a hero by some, and we've sold more papers than ever, he's....'

He pauses, then lowers his voice. 'I think whoever told him to keep it quiet is giving him a hard time, which means he's not in a good mood, so steer clear of him if you can.'

'Any idea who he was covering it up for?'

'People in high places, Beth. People who don't like their unethical and crooked ways of dealing with things exposed.'

'Are you thinking of...'

'Yes, why not? It's about time people know what this lot are really like. Corruption in high places isn't new, but exposing it is. They normally get away with it. They think they're above the law, but this time...'

'Where are you?'

'He sent me to Shepherd's Bush to cover that case.'

'Which case?'

'Three women murdered in the space of three weeks. It looks like ritual killings. They were tortured, then stuffed into cases.'

'Where were they found?'

'Behind the station, then another dumped in a car park. The last one was in a shop doorway. A nasty shock for the shop assistant who was told to open it by his boss.'

'They should've called the police.'

He grunts.

'It sounds like a serial killer, doesn't it?'

'Yes, Beth. Now, before I forget, did Sofia call you?'

'Yes, but I haven't had time to call her back.'

'Call her before you get on the train — keep in her good books. I think she likes you, then call me. By the way, you're covering this serial killer case with me.'

I'm just about to press her number when a call comes through from DI O'Hara.

'Beth, this is Detective O'Hara. Could you come to the station now?'

'Now?'

'Yes, if you can.'

'Is it about the man who attacked me?'

She laughs. 'We can discuss it when you're down here.'
'Right, I'll be there in about thirty minutes.'
'Good.'

CENTRAL LONDON POLICE Station

Just as before I walk across the park, pass the *Coach and Horses,* then in a few minutes I'm at Central London Police Station.

I'm shown to DI O'Hara's office — the door's already open, and she's sitting there waiting for me.

She waves me in. 'Take a seat. I'll be with you in a minute.'

She's sifting through a pile of papers, and I sit waiting, wondering what she's going to tell me.

Her twinkling blue eyes suddenly come to rest on my face. 'The last time you were here, I asked if you could think of anyone who would want to harm you from the story you are covering now?'

I nod.

'And you said with all those glass buildings at Canary Wharf, someone might see you talking to people close to the late Julia Ballantyne-Smythe?'

I nod. 'Do you know who it was?'

She sighs. 'You were right. You said either it was a coincidence him breaking into your place or someone paid him to do it.'

I nod.

Why doesn't she tell me? She must know who did it, otherwise why bring me down here?

She leans forward. 'That got me thinking. Two cases.

One a murder on the Tube. The other a break in at your apartment by someone with an awful lot of money on him. Immigration has no record of him entering the country. Then the detective handling the Tube murder case in Hampstead contacted me. She told me she knew you and could we meet.'

Aha, now this is making sense. I told Fred I'd seen DI O'Hara, and she'd told me the man who attacked me had a lot of money on him. She put two and two together and...

DI O'Hara's beaming at me now. 'You were right. After a little interrogation, the man who attacked you admitted being paid to break into your apartment and rough you up. Or rather, to put you out of action.'

A shiver runs down my spine. *I know what's coming.*

'It was none other than Olivia Marshall who paid him to do it, the wife of Allen Marshall who was having an affair with Julia Ballantyne - Smythe.'

'And did he admit to anything else?'

She nods. 'We found out where he'd been staying and searched his room. There was lots of cash stuffed under the floorboard. When questioned he said he'd won it gambling.'

'So...'

'I contacted DI Larson, who came to question him about the murder of Julia Ballantyne - Smythe. The case is in her jurisdiction and she's the detective covering it. When interviewed she told him we might go lighter on him if he told the truth.'

After what the redhead said about the north London detective who behaved like a nutter, I can understand how successful Sofia was when interrogating the guy who attacked me.

She leans back in her chair and smiles. 'Anyway, to cut a

long story short eventually, he told her. Olivia Marshal paid him to kill her and rough you up.'

She gets up and walks me to the door. 'Well, now you have your story, you can head back to your newsroom.'

'Yes and thank you. Thank you very much for all your help.'

'Thank you, Beth. We couldn't have done it without you.'

42

As soon as I'm out of the station, I walk along the street, take out my phone and call Fred. I must let him know what's happened.

'I know. Sofia told me all about it,' he replies. 'That's why I was trying to get hold of you last night. We have another breaking story.'

'So, the other day, when I went to the V&A...'

'Yes, and you were right — the guy had lots of money on him — someone paid him to do it. Even if you'd locked the door, he would've got into your apartment. You must get some bars put around that door, especially as it's happened before.'

He's right. I can't believe I thought a lock like that would keep people like him out.

'Beth, you have a story. A front-page story. I've already typed it up, and it's ready to send to the newsroom.'

It's all happening so fast and in a good way for a change.

'Fred, there's a text coming through from Sofia — I'll put you on hold while I read it.'

'Okay.'

We got her Beth, and I think your little genius has it all typed up ready for you to SEND.
  Sofia

I reply:

Will do, and thanks for all the help. We couldn't have done it without you.
  Beth

'Fred, are you still there?'
'Of course.'
'Send it, send it to Hardcastle.'
'With the greatest of pleasure, that should cheer him up. I'll be in the Coach and Horses in ten minutes, so get the drinks ready.'
'How did you know I was here?'
'DI O'Hara called Sofia and told her you'd just left, then Sofia called me.'

Coach and Horses

I'm at our table with a G&T, a Sauvignon Blanc and two packets of crisps. Fred will probably want to eat, but for now all I want is a glass of cold white wine and a bag of crisps.

'Another wine, Beth?'

I look up. It's PC Donnelly.

'No, thanks.'

'I heard you'd been to see DI O'Hara, and I knew you'd probably be here. Are you waiting for someone?'

'Fred's on his way, and I know he'd love to see you.'

She returns with her drink just as Fred walks through the door.

'PC Donnelly, how nice to see you.'

He walks over, gives her a hug, then sees his drink on the table, sits down, takes a gulp, then looks at her. 'Did you see the front-page news on our paper yesterday?'

She nods. 'Very good. I knew you'd do it. Oh, and by the way, I'm no longer a PC. I've risen in the ranks. I'm now a DC—detective constable.'

Fred raises his glass, and so do I.

Suddenly there's a shout and a clapping of hands from those sitting where the TV is on the other side of the pub.

We all go over to see what's happened.

Flashing across the screen are the words...

BREAKING NEWS - MINISTER RESIGNS

Fred's over the moon. He grabs hold of me — plants a big kiss on my cheek, then does the same to DC Donnelly.

In my ear he murmurs, 'We did it, Beth.'

'It wasn't me; it was all down to you.'

DC Donnelly looks over at the TV, then at us. 'This is a reaction to that fish market murder case, isn't it?'

Fred just grins. 'Thanks for letting us take a peek at that oyster crate before old Hardcastle arrived and having a chat with that fish market worker.'

She laughs. 'I'm amazed he printed the story.'

Fred and I exchange glances.

She rolls her eyes. 'Don't tell me. It was a case of gentle persuasion. No way would he do that willingly.'

Fred nods. 'Something like that. This calls for a celebration. What'll it be?'

'I wish I could, but I'm on duty. '

'Beth?'

'No, thanks.'

DC Donnelly gives me a sharp look. 'Everything alright, Beth?'

I nod. 'Yes, I just don't feel like drinking.'

She drains her glass and gets up. 'Well, I must love you and leave you. Do you need a lift?'

'Where are you going?' Fred asks.

'Back to the station.'

'No thanks, we're covering a story in Shepherd's Bush.'

After she's gone, he stands up. 'Beth, I think you need to go home and rest.'

'Do I look that bad?'

'No, you look great, but you've given Hardcastle another front-pager, so I don't think he'll be looking for you today.'

He calls for an Uber, drops me off outside my apartment, then carries on in the cab to Shepherd's Bush.

43

BAYSWATER

When I arrive home Mum's in the kitchen and Jamie's getting his stuff ready for school tomorrow.

She looks surprised to see me. 'Everything alright?'

I nod. 'Yes.'

She smiles. 'Good, I've made some coffee. Let's go into the living room. I have something to tell you that might interest you.'

She pours the coffee, then hands me one.

'You know about the Greek guy I met here, don't you?'

'Yes, Mum, you told me you might set up a business in Athens with him.'

That's also why I've been worried about Jamie being left alone when I'm at work, but I don't tell her that.

'You don't have to stay here now, you know, that don't you?'

I'm about to say something, but she holds up her hand.

'Yanni and I are going into business. We've been planning it for some time.'

'Doing what?'

'Food tours in Athens, and if you'd like to join us…'

Now I am surprised.

Mum carries on. 'You know a lot about Athens. The out of the way places to eat. Places most tourists never find. It would take your mind off things, and Jamie would be happy…'

I sit sipping my coffee thinking, what a great idea it is. She knows Athens like the back of her hand, and with her Greek friend Yanni to help, they should do well.'

'Well, what do you think?'

'There's too much going on, Mum, at the moment.'

'Like what?'

'Did Elias tell you about Dev?'

She frowns. 'No, what happened?'

'I can't say much because of who he works for…'

She nods. 'I know.'

'He's recovering somewhere here but wants to be alone. I just feel so…'

'No, Beth, don't go beating yourself up thinking of things that might or could have been. He's safe, and that's the main thing. If he needs time to himself — you of all people should understand that.'

She gives me a hug. 'Think it over, and don't worry, it only makes it worse.'

'I am worried, Mum. I have Jamie to think of as well. He loves Athens, but I don't think I could live there now. Too many memories…'

'You need a break, and I think I know just the place to go.'

Putting my mug on the table, I stand up. 'I'm still working, Mum. I'm covering a story with Fred.'

'Yes, but a couple of days by the sea will do you and Jamie good. Spend some time with him Beth, children grow up quickly.' She gives me a hug. 'I should know, shouldn't I? A couple of days in Cornwall will recharge your batteries, give you time to think. You used to love going there and Jamie loves it as well. Don't you have some days off owing to you?'

I walk into the kitchen.

How funny Mum should mention Cornwall. The last time I spoke to Dev, he mentioned liking Cornwall as a child. Maybe his parents had a house there?

Could Dev be in Cornwall?

Mum gets up, comes into the kitchen, and looks at me. 'So, what do you think?'

'I must call Elias. Be back in a minute.'

She looks surprised but says nothing.

His phone's ringing, then it goes to voicemail. I hang up. I need to talk to him, and if I'm right, at least I know where Dev is.

My phone flashes. It's Elias.

'Yes, Beth, is everything alright?'

'Yes, I was just thinking about the last time I spoke to Dev.'

He sighs. 'I told you, stop worrying.'

'No, listen. We were talking about going to live in Cornwall, and I think he has a house there...'

Silence.

'Elias?'

'Beth, I promised Dev, so even if you're right, I have no way of knowing where he is. Give it a couple of days, and Beth, stop thinking. I'll call you soon.'

He hangs up.

My first reaction is to call Fred. He'll know how to find out where he lives, if he doesn't already know.

I hit his number.

He answers immediately.

'I know Dev's in Cornwall, but I need his address.'

'If he wanted you to know, he'd have called you, or told Elias, wouldn't he?'

I say nothing, now I regret asking him.

'Beth, I know you're worried, but you know as well as I do that if you wanted to be left alone...'

I sigh.

'And after what they did to him...'

'You know, don't you?'

'No, but I can imagine. If you'd gone through what he has...' Then his voice softens. 'I know you're worried, but I'm sure he'll contact you when he's ready.'

'Fred, it's just that... well, he's always been there for me, and now he's hurt and I'm not there for him.'

'It rarely works that way. If I was in his position, I wouldn't want to see anyone until I'd recovered.'

'Yeah, as usual, you're right. I don't know what I'd do without you, Fred.'

'I don't know what I'd do without you, either Beth. Now have a rest or come to Shepherd's Bush and help me find this serial killer.'

44

TWO DAYS LATER
9.45pm

IT'S LATE. I spent today with Fred interviewing people about the serial killer case.

The serial killer case I covered before was nothing like this. Fred says he's covered many of these, so maybe he's not so shocked by them anymore, but it beats me how anyone can torture women in such a terrible way, and then shove them in a case. There are some sick people around, and it really makes you wonder what sort of world we're living in.

My phone rings, I let it ring. I've just spoken to Fred, and if it's Hardcastle, I don't want to speak to him.

Mum comes into the kitchen from the living room. 'Your phone's ringing. Don't you want to answer it?'

I'm standing looking out of the kitchen window. 'Not really. I've just spoken to Fred, and I don't want to speak to Hardcastle.'

Picking up my phone from the kitchen table, she smiles and walks over to me. 'I think you will. It's Dev.'

She hands me my phone, then goes into the living room.

'Dev. I've been so worried. Where are you?'

'Sorry I didn't call. I just haven't felt up to it.'

'Are you hurt badly?'

He laughs, cynically. 'I've still got all my bits and pieces. I'm still able to walk, although with a bit of a limp. Hopefully, with some help from physio I'll be back to my old self soon. I needed to rest and think. That's why I haven't called you.'

'Where are you?'

He laughs slightly. 'I spoke to Elias, and I think you know. You're quite good at this, aren't you, Beth? But there again, you're a reporter, and a very good one. I'm amazed you didn't find the address.'

I say nothing.

'I'm only joking. If you really want to come, I'll text you my address. It will take you about five or six hours by train.'

'Okay, I'll see you tomorrow.'

'Text me when you arrive at the station. I can get a cab to collect you.'

'Don't worry, I can get a cab, and I won't get there too early. Probably in the afternoon. See you tomorrow.'

'Bye, Beth.'

With a feeling of relief, I sit holding my phone, then I'm in the kitchen.

Mum looks up from making a tea. 'Is he alright?'

'I'm not sure. From what he said, he doesn't sound too bad, but I'll know more when I see him tomorrow.'

Mum's smiling. 'Tea or something to celebrate, maybe a glass of Cava?'

'A glass of Cava sounds good, Mum, but first I'll book my ticket to Cornwall.'

45

CORNWALL

I WAKE up and look out of the window.

It's Cornwall!

I must have dozed off for about an hour — I slept very little last night.

I had lots to think about and wonderful views of the passing scenery to look at, but I just couldn't keep my eyes open.

The train's just about to pull into the station and I'm feeling slightly nervous. It was a lovely journey—I haven't done that for a long time. The motion of the train always used to send me to sleep when I was a child and it still does, so I always end up missing half the journey.

I had too much to think about last night, plus I was worried I wouldn't wake up in time. Needless to say I shouldn't have worried because my alarm went off and Mum was already in the kitchen making coffee when I got up.

With my large shoulder bag and a bag of things I bought from the deli opposite — just a few Greek things I know Dev likes, I go exploring for a cab to take me to where Dev lives.

There's a taxi rank outside the station.

After giving the address to the driver, he nods and opens the back door.

I slide inside, close the door, and sit thinking of Dev. The name of the house is *High Trees,* so with a name like that, I wonder if there are lots of trees around it.

It feels a little strange meeting Dev like this. Usually, we meet in pubs, hotels in London or he collects me in his car. It's the same in Athens, I suppose. I've never taken a trip on a train to see him. This is a first.

The cab slows down, then it's in front of me. A lovely house surrounded by tall trees.

I pay the cab driver, then slide out onto the narrow road. There's a gentle breeze from the sea, the sound of seagulls, then the scent of the sea hits me.

As I walk closer to the house, I can see it's on top of a small cliff overlooking a small bay. I wonder if there's a way down to the beach from here. If there is, it must be lovely in the summer.

As I open the gate and walk along the path, the door opens and there's Dev. He must've heard the cab.

He looks very slim. And as I get closer; I can see the scars on his face.

My heart beats fast...

'Beth, so you found it?'

He steps back into the hallway so I can walk inside, then closes the door.

I look around. It's a very comfortable house full of character but modern inside more than outside. It's the type of house I'd love to live in.

Dev walks with me into the living room. He walks slowly; he has a limp, and instead of his suit that he lives in most of the time, he's now wearing soft beige trousers and a black top.

As soon as I enter the room, I'm drawn to the fantastic view of the sea.

Suddenly, a woman with red curly hair comes into the room.

She smiles at Dev. 'Is there anything I can get you?'

'Sally, this is Beth.'

Sally smiles. I can see she's looking me up and down and taking me all in.

'Nice to meet you, Beth. Is there anything you'd like to drink?'

There's a slight accent. It must be Cornish.

'A coffee if it's not too much trouble.'

'No trouble at all.'

She looks at Dev.

'Same for me, Sally, and bring some of those croissants. I'm sure Beth hasn't eaten yet.'

'I'll bring you your pills. You need to take them now.'

She leaves the room and I'm left wondering who she is.

Dev sits on a dark green, comfortable looking sofa and points to another next to him. 'Sit down, Beth.'

I sit just looking at him. He looks so pale and much thinner than he usually is. I want to run over and hug him, but I don't.

'You've been through a lot, Dev.'

'Yes, and it's my own bloody fault. I should've stayed in London or at least gone back to Athens. I won't be going on anymore missions now, that's for sure.'

His penetrating blue eyes come to rest on my face. He smiles. 'I'll stay here for a while till I'm back on track.'

Sally comes into the room, places coffee and croissants in front of me, then gives Dev his coffee, plus a small bowl containing pills and a glass of water.

After she's gone he looks at me, pops a pill into his mouth, swallows it with water then smiles. 'You're wondering who she is, aren't you?'

I nod.

'She's the daughter of the housekeeper who used to look after the house for my parents. She lives in the village with her husband and children. When she heard I was here and saw the state I was in, she offered to come and help.'

I say nothing, just sit watching him.

'I'd already contacted the local doctor to see if a nurse could pop in from time to time, which she does, so it seemed a good idea. I've known her family for a long time and the money comes in handy for her.'

I shake my head. 'You should've called me, I could've...'

'You have your job, Beth. You have your son to look after.'

'Still, you should've called me.'

'What about your job and Jamie?'

'He was with Mum in Athens, and now she's with him in London, but she'll be going back to Athens soon. She's starting a business with a Greek friend of hers...'

He says nothing, just sits watching me.

'Jamie loves Athens, but he knows I can't live there at the moment. I told him and he understands.'

Our eyes meet. I walk over and sit on the arm of the sofa. 'I want to be with you, but Jamie needs to get used to us being together. On the way here I thought if he could spend the weekends here — get to know you — then he'll get used to us being together.'

'And your job?'

'I have to work a month's notice, so I'll ask Mum if she can delay going to Athens.'

His arms are around my waist, then I'm on the seat next to him. He draws me to him, we kiss, then he draws away and winces slightly. 'I'm still not healed, so you must be patient, okay?'

I want to know what happened but won't ask—it's up to him if he wants to tell me. The trauma he's been through isn't only physical, he might need a little more than just physio to get him back on track.

46

HIGH TREES
 Cornwall

DEV LOOKS AT ME. 'I'm sorry about Helen. I know how much she meant to you.'

I freeze. I don't reply.

He turns and looks at me. 'You don't think it was an accident, do you?'

'No.'

'Do you want to go to Spain?'

I shake my head, but I can see he's not convinced.

'You nearly didn't make it when you were up that mountain road, remember?'

I nod.

He frowns. 'When I was in that hellhole in North Africa, I thought…'

A muscle twitches in his cheek. His face is a mask. 'If I get out of here, I don't want to spend the rest of my life on missions anymore. With the time I have left, I want to enjoy life, not spend it flying around the world risking my life for...'

He turns and looks at me. 'We're not here for long, so why not make the most of it and be happy?'

His words send a shiver down my spine.

'What is it, Beth?'

'Helen said that the last time she called me. I was busy getting ready for work. She said she couldn't understand why I was still slogging away at my job when...'

Getting up, I walk over to the window. 'They took it away from her,' I murmur, then swing round and look at Dev. 'Helen had so much to live for and those bastards—'

He's on his feet. 'You know you can't go there now, don't you?'

'I...'

Then I stop. I'm about to tell him I already went.

He pulls me to him. 'You've been lucky so far, Beth, and so have I.' He turns my face to his. 'Let's sit down, have your coffee, eat something and tell me what's been happening.'

So, we sit and talk. I tell him about our latest story to hit the headlines but leave out the bit about the man attacking me in my apartment.

His phone rings.

He answers.

I get up to leave him to talk and walk over to the window. What a lovely place to come to! He couldn't have chosen a better place, and it's his home, so he can relax and hopefully get better soon. Although it's not summer, the sea looks lovely and the beach...

'Beth.'

'Yes.'

'That was David.'

I draw in a deep breath.

He comes over and stands beside me staring out at the view of the sea, then he turns to me. 'You should have told me. Why didn't you?'

'Told you what?'

He looks angry.

Shit, now what!

A muscle twitches in his cheek. His face is stony.

I go to walk away. He grabs me, then winces with pain. 'You know very well what I mean,' he mutters. 'If we are to have any chance of a life together, I must trust you.'

'Okay, I went to Spain. I was angry. I wanted to see where it happened.'

'Yes, and they nearly killed you.'

Has David told him about Miguel?

His voice softens slightly. 'I know you Beth and you don't give up, but this time you must. You have no chance with them. These people are evil and cruel. You must promise me you'll never go back there.'

I swallow. *How can I promise something like that?*

He sits down on the sofa. He looks tired. I go over and hug him. 'I won't, okay?'

'Promise?'

I nod.

'Say it.'

'I won't go back while they're there.'

He gives a cynical smile. 'You're always optimistic, aren't you, Beth?'

Before I can reply, there's a tap at the door. It's Sally.

'Yes, Sally?'

'Elias is here.'

Elias walks in, comes over, hugs me, then Dev. 'I had to come to see how you are. I hope you don't mind me arriving like this.'

Dev looks happy. 'It's good to see you, Elias. How long are you staying?'

'I can stay for a few days if that's alright.'

'Good.'

Dev looks at me. 'When are you going back to London, Beth?'

'Tomorrow morning. I have things to arrange.'

Elias interrupts. 'I can book in at the local pub in the village.'

'We have five bedrooms, so there are more than enough.'

Sally's watching us. 'I'll make up the beds, then.'

Elias turns to her. 'I need to put my case somewhere. Is it possible for you to show me where I can leave it?'

'Of course, follow me.'

Dev sits looking at me, then smiles. 'You have it all worked out, don't you?'

'Not really. I'm just trying very hard to make things work for all of us.'

'So next weekend your mum and Jamie will come and stay here?'

I nod. 'If that's alright with you?'

I walk over, and he pulls me to him. 'I missed you Beth, being in that place made me realize...'

I lean over and kiss him. 'I'll be back soon.'

'What if Jamie doesn't like it?'

'I already checked the schools in the area, and I think, in fact, I know, he'll be much happier here than in London.'

He frowns. 'Well, it sounds good, but what about our detective agency? Cornwall or London?'

'We can start with a small office and apartment above it in London to work from and another here... or we can look for a place to work from in Truro. That's not too far from here, is it?'

Dev looks amazed.

'Then whichever works best...'

'But how can we possibly do that? There are only two of us, Beth.'

'We try Cornwall first, and if that doesn't work, we get one in London. We'll have an apartment and run the agency from there.'

'A lot to think about,' he mutters.

The door opens and in comes Elias. 'How about if I cook dinner tonight? Anyone fancy Greek food?'

I smile. 'Now that's a really great idea, Elias.'

Dev laughs. 'As long as you don't mind cooking it. There's beer in the fridge and everything you need in the kitchen. Get a beer and a snack, then come and tell us what's been happening in Athens and bring some nibbles for us to eat.'

'Such as?' asks Elias.

'Olives, cheese, anything to nibble on till the food's ready.'

'Oh, I forgot.' I take out the cakes and sausages I bought from the Greek deli that I know Dev loves. 'Can you put these in the kitchen for me, Elias?'

He takes them from me. 'Tonight, I will make something Dev really likes. And for you Beth, I'll make a Greek vegan meal.'

He goes off whistling to the kitchen, and Dev turns to me.

'Are you going to call your mum or wait till you get back to London to see if she can stay a few more weeks with Jamie?'

'I'll call her later, while you and Elias are catching up with things about Athens.'

'Does Jamie know you've come to see me in Cornwall?'

'I didn't tell him because it was late when you called, but Mum will tell him today. It's funny, but before I knew you were here, Mum suggested coming to Cornwall for a weekend break. Actually, it was when she said that I remembered talking to you about Cornwall and asking if you'd been here.'

He shakes his head and tussles my hair. 'My little detective, I think we'll be alright. You with your skills and me...'

He looks down at his body, sighs, then asks.

'Jamie likes it here, doesn't he?'

'Yes, he loves Cornwall.'

'And the business your mum's thinking of starting in Athens with her Greek friend — do you know what it is?'

'Yes, in fact, she asked me to join them if I wanted to.'

'Doing what?'

'Food tours, taking tourists to the out of the way places to sample Greek food at traditional Greek restaurants and bars.'

Now Dev's laughing. 'Ask Elias to join them. I once told him he should write a book on all the places he knows to get good Greek food at reasonable prices.'

'Yes, but then all the tourists will get to know of them.'

'True.'

Suddenly, his face is serious. 'It's good Elias is here to keep me company. It will stop me from thinking.'

'Yes, exactly what I was thinking. He's so laid back, he enjoys cooking and playing Tavli. And when you're tired, you just go for a lay down like he does. Mum loves Cornwall, so she'll be looking forward to coming to see you as well.'

The door opens and in comes Elias carrying a tray of about ten plates of tasty bites to eat, ranging from dolmades to bits of cheese.

'Wow, that looks good, Elias.'

He gives me a wink. 'With me here, Dev's going to put on a few pounds.'

Elias walks over to the round table and arranges the small dishes of food then returns to the kitchen for drinks.

Dev suddenly pulls me to him. 'I want you in my bed with me tonight, but the state I'm in...'

The living room door opens and Elias returns with some beers and cokes.

I lean over and kiss Dev and murmur. 'Let's eat some of Elias's Greek mezedes.'

THE END

If you enjoyed this book please don't forget to rate and leave a short review **here.**

And to see what happens next...
Check out Book 10 — **Hidden From View**

BOOK 1 : FOLLOWED SAMPLE
A BETH PAPADAKIS CRIME THRILLER

London, Paddington Station
Early September

THE BUS SWAYS around Marble Arch, turns left onto Edgware Road, screeches to a halt at a bus stop where about ten people are waiting and I sit wondering if I'll catch my train. I wanted to stop off at Evesly to check on Helen's house, but now I probably won't make it.

The door's slam shut, the bus gathers speed. No more stopping at stops, as we're already overloaded. *If it carries on at this, I might just make my train.*

A few minutes later, we're outside Paddington Tube Station. Leaping off the bus, I sprint across the street—a cyclist curses me; I ignore him, run down the small side street into London Paddington train station and look frantically for the overhead board.

Someone nudges me. It's a guy of about eighteen. He turns and gives me a big smile. 'It's over there, the board's over there!' Then he turns and runs to catch his train.

I run over to scan the board. *London to Oxford leaving in two minutes.* The station's heaving with people—*will I make it?*

Running as fast as I can I reach the platform in one minute—swipe my ticket over the automatic barrier—run and jump on the train, which looks practically empty, flop down on one of the pale blue seats and breathe a sigh of relief.

The whistle blows, doors close - the train clanks and groans its way out of Paddington station and I sit gazing at the passing warehouses and rows of old terraced houses, glad to be leaving London.

What a terrible interview that was, such a waste of time. All they wanted was someone to dish the dirt—be a newspaper gossip columnist.

'Mind if I sit here?'

There's a scruffy-looking guy peering into my face. He points to the seat beside me.

I turn and look around.

There's an elderly man at the far end of the carriage reading his newspaper. Other than him, the carriage is empty.

IN TOO DEEP

I gesture to the rows of empty seats. 'There are lots of seats over there.'

He just ignores me and plonks himself down, stretches out his long thin legs, wriggles as if getting himself comfortable, then gives me a sly sideway look.

'No, I'd rather sit here.'

His voice is weird, quite high pitched. He has watery blue eyes, a droopy looking brown moustache and limp, greasy brown hair.

What a shit day and now this idiot to deal with. If I was on the Tube, I could understand it. People pressed together like sardines, the stench of body odor, stale breath, unwanted bodily contact—you're lucky if you can find a seat. But this train is empty.

He sits staring at me. He has a horrible sneer on his face. It's as if he's challenging me to say something. Without looking at him, I get up and walk through the train.

I'll find another seat with people nearby.

An hour later, the train pulls into Oxford. This is where I should get off, but I'm going to Helen's house, so I change platforms and wait for the train to Evesly. It's a lovely day— it'll only take twenty minutes to get there. Her parents died in a car accident a year ago and she hasn't been back since it happened. I glance at my phone. I have just enough time to check on her house, then I'll collect Jamie from school.

A few minutes later, the train arrives, but unlike the train from London, this one is quite busy. No more empty carriages for me today. There's a window seat vacant next to a woman with a baby, which I quickly grab.

Fields of corn and honey colored Cotswold stone houses flash by the train's window reminding me of when I lived here, it's where I met Helen. We used to take the shortcut home most days after school—it was at the back of the station. I sit thinking about those two years—*I wonder if the shortcut's still there?*

Twenty minutes later, I'm outside Evesly station. Nothing much has changed—it all looks the same as the last time I was here. It's a typical sleepy little Cotswold village where everyone knows each other. Mum and dad worked at a college in Oxford for a couple of years, then Dad's mum became ill, so we went back to Athens.

Throwing my jacket over my shoulder, I walk around to the back of the station. The path's still here. It's a bit overgrown, but on a day like this, who wants to take the bus when it's just a ten-minute walk to Helen's house.

I stroll along the overgrown pathway, inhaling the familiar scent of wildflowers and corn. It's early September, so a lovely time to be in the country, especially on such a warm sunny day. Blackberry bushes are heavy with fruit—I stop to pick one, they still taste good.

After a few minutes of walking, I stop.

I have the weirdest feeling I'm being followed.

I turn to look, but nobody's there.

I walk faster.

Soon I can see the top of Helen's house, not far to go, just a few minutes and I'll be there.

The sound of a twig snapping makes me freeze. *I'm not imagining it.* Then, to my horror, someone laughs.

I swing round. 'What's so damn funny?'

Before I can see who it is, something's thrown over my head—I try pulling it off, but it's too tight.

I kick out quickly as hard as I can.

'Fucking bitch!' he screams.

My arms are behind me in a vice-like grip. I try to fight him off, but he's caught me off balance, he's pushing me down on the ground. One of his hands is up my skirt. It's inside my pants. His grip on my other arm isn't so strong now—he's too busy trying to pull my pants down.

I quickly turn and kick him.

He lets out a shriek of pain.

Pulling the cloth off my face, I see him clutching his crotch.

He raises his eyes to me and lunges forward.

I kick him again, this time in the face.

He falls back, blood streaming from his nose.

Hauling himself up, he makes a run for it.

He's about three yards away, then he stops, turns, glares at me and shouts.

'You wait, you bitch, I'll get you for this.'

I stand transfixed. I know who it is; it's the guy from the train, the one who sat next to me. For a second I watch as he crawls through the hedge, then I run after him.

Buy it on Amazon FREE in Kindle Unlimited!

BOOK 2 : THE KILLING
LONDON CRIME THRILLER SERIES

She's a journalist, she's no stranger to the darker side of life, so when Beth leaves the icy cold weather of London to head for the warmer shores of Athens to cover the political situation, she's looking forward to a few days in the sun and meeting up with old friends. However, that's not what happens.

Just hours after arriving in Athens, she's having lunch with a friend who's behaving strangely...

Eventually, her friend tells Beth what's wrong. A mutual friend who's a reporter didn't show up last night as arranged. No phone call or text message to say he wasn't coming, which is out of character. As well as not answering his calls, nobody's seen him since yesterday afternoon, not even his wife.

Later, when Beth's in the bar of her hotel, she notices the headlines of a local newspaper tell of a shooting outside a bar by the beach. Could this have something to do with their missing friend?

A lawyer friend of Helen's offers to help. He's a close friend of their missing friend James, but unbeknown to Helen and Beth, he also works for MI6.

Book 2 - *THE KILLING* is a political crime thriller that takes you on a journey from London to the Athenian Riviera and the streets of the old town.

Available on Amazon FREE in Kindle Unlimited!

BOOK 3 : PANIC

A SUICIDE BOMB ATTACK ON THE LONDON TUBE, A RUTHLESS HUMAN TRAFFICKING RING IN SPAIN...

She's a reporter, but she needs a change, so when her friend, who works for MI6, says she should apply for a job working with him, and she's tempted...

It's something she's always wanted to do, but she needs to think — she needs to decide what's best for her and her son Jamie

A short Easter weekend break by the sea will give her the time she needs to decide what to do. So whilst her MI6 friend Dev is fighting off terrorist attacks in London, she heads for the warmer shores of Spain's Costa Tropical and her friend's hotel.

Late one night while driving along the coastal road in Malaga, she comes face to face with criminal activities on the beach. Switching off her headlights, she pulls over, and then, to her horror, she realizes she knows someone who seems in charge of what's happening. Even worse, he's seen her watching him...

From this moment on, she's trapped in the dark underbelly of organized crime in Spain. Can she escape from their clutches? Will the person she knows who's involved in this help her?

This very dark crime thriller takes you from London to the treacherous mountain roads and vibrant streets of Granada, along the sandy beaches of the Costa del Sol to La Linea drug capital of Spain.

PANIC **is Book 3 in the fast-paced London Crime Thriller Series.**

Available on Amazon FREE in Kindle Unlimited!

BOOK 4 : PAYBACK

BETH PAPADAKIS DOESN'T GO LOOKING FOR TROUBLE, BUT TROUBLE ALWAYS SEEMS TO FINDS HER...

Beth leaves the safety of London to help her friend Helen and returns to Spain but ends up getting more involved in the dangerous world of drug and people trafficking.

On her journey, she travels from the treacherous mountain roads and streets of Granada to the sandy beaches of the Costa del Sol.

She becomes emotionally involved and meets women brought illegally to Spain to work in the sex trade and those being forced to work for one of the most vicious drug kingpins.

While all this is happening, her friend Dev, who works for MI6, is working with Interpol to bring a stop to the illicit drug and people trafficking into Southern Spain.

When he discovers Beth's trying to help people escape from a ruthless people trafficker, he tries to stop her, but she's in too deep. Her life's now in terrible danger.

PAYBACK is book 4 in the fast-paced London Crime Thriller Series.

Available on Amazon FREE in Kindle Unlimited!

BOOK 5 : PURE EVIL

AN EDGE OF YOUR SEAT THRILLER SET IN LONDON…

This dark, fast-paced crime thriller involves corruption in high places and draws you into the ruthless underbelly of organized crime in London's Mayfair.

Beth's back at work, but she's reporting on crime, not politics. Her new boss says he'll ease her in gently, but that's not what happens.

Still struggling emotionally and physically from the recent events in Spain, Beth's thrown in at the deep end. First there's the body of a young woman in Hyde Park, then a shooting takes place outside a casino in London's Mayfair.

Beth's sent to cover the Mayfair shooting of a popular croupier who, it seems, was involved with an MP. Her boss wants results, and he wants them now! Who murdered the two young women who met their untimely deaths in London's Mayfair?

Now it's up to Beth to deliver, and she does. She get's right into the hornet's nest and the organized crime scene in London, but what she discovers is so terrible - even worse, her life's now in danger.

PURE EVIL **is Book 5 in the exciting Beth Papadakis crime thriller series.**

Buy it on Amazon ~ FREE in Kindle Unlimited!

BOOK 6 : FALLOUT
AN EXCITING EDGE OF YOUR SEAT THRILLER...

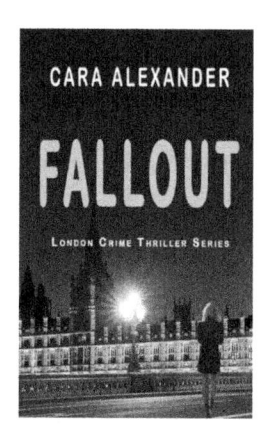

A story that's ripped out of the headlines...

Beth's sent to cover a terrorist attack in London's Westminster, but within minutes of arriving at the scene, things go horribly wrong.

She's abducted and forced at gunpoint to go with the terrorists, and her colleague Fred gets shot in the leg.

Did he see what happened to Beth?

Is there a mole in Westminster? Was it an inside job?

Then someone viciously kills two detectives who Beth is close to—does this have something to do with the terrorist attack?

While all this is happening Dev, who works for MI6, is on his way from Paris to help with the attacks in London, but will he get there in time to help Beth and Fred?

FALLOUT is Book 6 in the exciting London Crime Thriller Series.

Buy on Amazon FREE in Kindle Unlimited!

BOOK 7 : FATAL INTENT

Beth's back on the crime beat in this dark, fast-paced thriller. She's sent to cover a potential serial killer case in north London — two women are dead — is there going to be a third?

Her boss wants results, but this time he's given Beth a deadline.
 Her colleague Fred's covering a hotel killing in

London's Mayfair, which eventually proves disastrous for him and Beth.

While Beth's up to her neck in organized crime in London, her friend Dev, who works for MI6, surprises her by saying he's being transferred to the Middle East and wants her to go with him.

Buy now on Amazon FREE in Kindle Unlimited!

A crime thriller based in London, *FATAL INTENT* is Book 7 in the exciting London Crime Thriller Series.

BOOK 8 : NEMESIS
A DARK FAST PACED CRIME THRILLER...

Beth's back on the crime beat in London when she gets an urgent message to go to Athens... but a big story's about to break in the UK and her boss wants results today, not tomorrow!

> This could be the scoop of the year for him. He wants his best investigative reporters covering it, which means Beth and Fred.

Beth's had a lot of experience with drug and people trafficking in Spain, and Fred's a genius at hacking into computers.

She has no choice but to take the next flight to Athens, but what she discovers when she gets there is terrible.

She's now in the dark underbelly of organized crime in Athens, hunting for a killer. Can her colleague Fred cover for her while she's in Athens?

Buy now on Amazon FREE in Kindle Unlimited

NEMESIS is Book 8 in the dark, fast-paced London Crime Thriller Series.

BOOK 10 : HIDDEN FROM VIEW
BETH PAPADAKIS DOESN'T GO LOOKING FOR TROUBLE, BUT TROUBLE ALWAYS SEEMS TO FIND HER...

Beth's back on the crime beat In this dark and gritty crime thriller... She's on a brief visit to Cornwall to see MI6 friend Dev, when she stumbles upon a murdered woman in the cove below his house with echoes of her past encounters in Spain.

Dev's health worsens and Beth's in a dilemma. Torn between loyalty to him and her journalistic instincts, she defies his pleas to leave the investigation to the local police and goes in search of the woman's killer.

Meanwhile, shocking revelations from her colleague Fred in London intensify the race against time, forcing Beth to navigate the treacherous balance between personal loyalty and the duty to expose the sinister web of human trafficking.

Hidden from View **is Book 10 in the dark, fast-paced London Crime Thriller Series with crime reporter Beth Papadakis.**

Buy on Amazon FREE in Kindle Unlimited!

FREE BOOK GIVEAWAY
THE PREQUEL

Click here to receive a FREE digital copy of BREAKUP
the prequel to the London Crime Thriller Series.
Or visit my website at **www.caraaalexander.com**
and sign up to my **VIP Club** and be the first to get all the
news, previews and lots of other cool deals.

Never miss a new release...

I usually email once a month unless I have something really good to tell you.

No spam, ever, guaranteed. You can unsubscribe at any time.

ABOUT THE AUTHOR

I live in London at the moment, but I've lived in many other countries including Spain and Greece, which appear in a few of the books in the London Crime Thriller Series.

If you have any comments or questions about the books just contact me via my website or on my FB page as I'd love to hear from you.

You can follow me on FB for all the latest news about books and special offers...

Facebook.com/caraalexanderauthor

And sign up to my VIP Club for my monthly newsletter :

https://www.caraalexander.com

For my Family with love

Printed in Great Britain
by Amazon